I0534425

The Ones
We Love

Jonathan Sayer

ISBN-13: 979-8-9912826-1-1

The Ones We Love

Cover inspired by: Denny McCoy

Designed by: Jonathan Sayer

Printed in the United States of America.

Praise for *The Ones We Love*

"A fun, easy read!"

- *JOHN PIERSON, FILM PRODUCER AND AUTHOR OF "SPIKE, MIKE, SLACKERS, & DYKES."*

"This is a well written, thought-provoking book. The complex, non-judgmental assemblage of various ages, settlers, law officers, and 'Indians and Outlaws' works well."

- *DR. WILLIAM R. KINNEY, PROF. EMERITUS, UT/AUSTIN & MEMBER OF THE CHICKASAW NATION.*

"I was delightfully surprised when I found myself turning pages faster and faster... Highly recommended."

- *BETTE LEE CROSBY, BEST SELLING AUTHOR OF 26 NOVELS.*

"Totally Impressed. It's a true page-turner and I loved the ending."

- *BARRY DAVIS, LONG-TIME PUBLISHING INDUSTRY EXECUTIVE.*

For Lesa, Audrey, and Evan

PREFACE

The Ones We Love is set in a period of the United States when the post-Civil War policies of Reconstruction and Western Expansion have shattered the traditions of proud indigenous peoples. The novel's journey transpires just as the remnants of these long-established communities become overwhelmed by an intentional strategy of violence and starvation. Their children are often assimilated into government schools, and those broken families that remain are forced far afield to settle on unfamiliar federal reservations.

The Ones We Love

CHAPTER 1

IN THE EARLY hours of the day, before I knew much about killing, Pa asked me to come with him and Mister Coates to town. It was a cold morning of my fifteenth year in 1873. Mister Coates sat up front in the buckboard with Pa. I rode in back, bouncing on a pile of empty feed sacks, cradling Pa's shotgun, and watching my dog chase after us across the lower pasture, yapping all the while.

Pa paused our two mules beneath a line of tall, bare cottonwood trees that stood beside the crick bordering our property. "Your mother wasn't pleased when I told her you'd be riding along, Mae." He said this with a glance at me over his shoulder. "She made sure to mention the list of chores you're supposed to be doing."

"Ma always has a list," I said as I looked down at the gun in my lap. The notion I'd abandoned Ma and my obligations for a little fun churned in the pit of my belly.

Pa's eyes sparkled. He grinned at Mister Coates beside him,

who chuckled. "Your mama gave me one of them too, Miss Mae. Though surely not as long."

I gazed at my dog again, wishing to laugh along with them, but thinking only of my ma. Her hands and forearms powdered in flour before the sun rose, shoving a pan of rolled biscuits into our hot cook stove with a hard thump that spoke of her aggravation.

"Go on," Ma had said, me feeling that guilt but unwilling to let go of my chance to participate in a few small adventures. Except for church, such a trip into town didn't come but once a month for Pa and was a rare thing for the likes of a farmer's daughter. The prospect of going blossomed in my mind and made me smile. Different sights and sounds for a change — if only witnessed from the back of our open wagon on the double-track trail that led to Weld.

Pa made a clicking sound out the side of his mouth and flicked his switch to get old Janey and Cobb started through the icy water. Them mules dug deep and snorted as they pulled us up the muddy ruts on the far side. My dog barked a few more times and ran back towards the house until I couldn't see him no more beyond the cottonwoods.

Puffs of vapor came out of Pa and Mister Coates' mouths as they spoke of little things while we rolled along. Pa wanted to add planks of pine to the floor in Ma's kitchen. Mister Coates reminded him that the posts between the high and low pastures needed mending.

The wagon jolted, and I looked up at the sky. It was a pale blue and the sun white, no longer warm and yellow. The green of the broad, rolling prairie all around us had gone gray – dormant grass and scrub brush as far as the eye could see.

I shivered and wrapped my arms around my skirts and blanket, pulling my knees to my chest with Pa's gun tucked inside, hoping it would somehow make me warmer.

"You alright, Mae?"

I nodded when Pa asked, keeping his gaze on the mules he was driving. "Thank you again… for inviting me," I said between bumps and bounces, wanting to still sound delighted to be along for the ride. Course, inside I was wishing I'd worn my woolens.

"Bring another blanket next time. We got us a long time until spring," Pa said with a stern kindness. The sort that disclosed how well he knew me. He made the clicking sound again and Janey and Cobb shifted into a trot, pulling us on over the six rutted miles to town.

Weld was a muddy place. With only one true street, our unpainted church was set to the east, a boarding house stood all the way west at the opposite end. We passed the land office, a livery, blacksmith, and saloon – these made up most of the in-between. Them mules seemed to know where we were going. Janey and Cobb paused as soon as we pulled in front of the freshly whitewashed Crenshaw Mercantile where Pa set the brake.

Mister Coates didn't move when daddy swung down. He'd wait with me since he wasn't allowed inside. "Might be a good idea if you got something for Ma," I said to Pa as he handed Mister Coates his switch. Me thinking all the while about the likely heat of Ma's mood by the time we rolled back to the farm.

"I do have a plan," he said with a wink, squeezing my shoulder.

Pa tipped his hat at a feller and his lady who passed between him and the mercantile and then pushed his way in, making the bell on the door chime. With daddy inside, Mister Coates stepped down and took a ragged piece of cigarette out of his pocket, holding the stub between his thumb and finger like it was a thing of beauty. I stood in the bed of the wagon and tried to rub some of the ache out of my bum.

Mister Coates chuckled. "Maybe we ought to get you a better throne to sit on?"

I'm sure I scowled. "I ain't no princess."

He said nothing more, but I could tell he was still amused, watching me collect the feed sacks to shape a better seat. I plunked down again with the shotgun across my knees.

People in town were coming and going about their business same as us. A man in a flop hat and worn coat pushed a barrow full of manure on by. Two more in dungarees drove a team of four oxen the opposite way, dragging a long post through the

3

muck towards the livery. Not long after, Mister Coates and I laughed as three ducks waddled past - the trio clucking and exclaiming about everything they saw as if they'd traveled to town for some adventure as well.

"What are we buying today?" I said in a moment between so many passers-by.

Mister Coates lit his stub. He leaned against the wagon and took a puff. "Usual. Sundries, flour, corn meal for winter. Like your pappy says, it's a long time until spring."

Three men and a boy on horseback ambled past. The men were bundled in long coats and wide-brim hats. Their leather boots, shoved into tight stirrups, were caked with the mud that stuck to everything. The boy, not older than me, was wrapped in a blanket. All of them stared at Mister Coates before looking my way. Mister Coates averted his eyes, but I kept watching.

"Girl looks plain. Not very pretty," the biggest rider announced to the others as he took me in with his gaze. Man had a pale face and a ginger beard. Rode high in his saddle. The butt of a rifle poked out from beneath a fold in his coat. His words stung and the pleasure of our visit to town all but drained away. Made me look down at the pleats of my faded dress and Pa's shotgun still in my lap.

The boy in the blanket laughed while another man with a squeaky voice replied: "Keep you warm either way, Little John." The big man grunted, and I looked up at him again. He tipped his hat, eyeing me like his gesture weren't no apology and the four proceeded to move on.

"Don't you mind them, Miss Mae. Foul men with no proper manners," Mister Coates said in a hushed voice.

I kept my sight on the riders. Least until they swung their horses towards the prairie and disappeared at the edge of town. Trouble followed men like those with abundance.

Pa returned soon after, when he and the merchant began hauling out our provisions. I shook off my gloom and jumped out of the wagon to help. Mister Coates and I put the load in back with planks of wood for Ma's kitchen, half a dozen big sacks and twice as many smaller ones. After it was all arranged and set in the wagon, Pa handed me a small wooden box. Delicate and light as a feather. So tiny it fit in the palm of my hand.

"Open it," he said. "It's for your ma."

Inside, nestled against a soft tuft of cotton was a locket. Polished silver with a brass catch. I released the hook to lift the cover. Underneath was an image of Ma and Pa. They looked young and determined. Handsome and beautiful. I ran my finger across their familiar faces.

"Two newlyweds," Pa remarked with a distant look in his eyes.

In that moment I was proud of my pa and pleased again that I'd come along. Amused by his secret scheme to arrange such a special gift for Ma.

"I've never seen this photograph before. Where'd you get it?"

"A man's got to keep a few treasures to himself, Mae. You think she'll like it?"

I knew Ma would love it, nearly as much as she loved Pa. I gave him a hug and kissed him on the cheek. Pa held me in his arms a moment before slipping the box into the deep pocket of his coat.

We'd traveled halfway back from Weld when the tenor of our trip changed. The pale sun disappeared, covered by a shroud of gray clouds. The grass and scrub of the broad prairie became even more lifeless and dull than before.

"Mister Coates?" I said, narrowing my eyes at a rise in the distance.

Pa glanced back when he heard my voice but went on driving. He snapped the reins in his hands, keeping them mules going. Mister Coates chuckled. He pulled the collar of his coat closer about his neck and turned to acknowledge me. "Your bum still aching, Miss Mae?"

When he realized where my sight was drawn, he shifted to see what I was watching.

"Them fellers we saw in town," I said. "Ain't that them?"

Pa spotted them now too.

Four horses stood partially hidden by the crest of a rise between our wagon and the balance of the way home. Their riders looked down, watching us approach – three men and a boy. I knew there was nothing out here for them to seek, nothing but us and our small farm. A shade of dread began to prick at my thoughts.

Pa raised his hand to acknowledge the riders – something he'd do to anyone he met on the prairie. Mister Coates squinted to get a better sense of what we were rolling up to.

"No reason to wave Pa. Nothing nice about those men," I said quick, recalling what the big man had said and how he and the others had gazed upon me.

"That's them alright," confirmed Mister Coates. "Those men made fun of your daughter, Mister Kepler. Suggested Miss Mae wasn't… well..." He glanced at me again and dropped the subject.

The riders must not have liked Pa's hello-wave. They retreated their horses, moving more out of our sight, using the slope for cover, before the big one with the beard led them the rest of the way. The men and that one boy were gone as quick as they'd appeared.

"Mae… pass Mister Coates the shotgun."

"I know how to use it."

"No doubt, Mae. You are good with it. But right now, I need you to do as I say." Pa's voice was sharp, not angry; I heard a thread of fear within it.

I handed Mister Coates the gun. He had a better spot to see the trail ahead up there with Pa. I raised myself on my knees so I could get a look too as we rattled along, but by the time we came to where them horses had been standing, the riders had vanished.

"Tracks lead to the scrub," observed Mister Coates. Four sets of horse hooves marked a path into the low brush and tangled junipers that crowded close along this stretch of the trail.

"What do they want, Pa?"

He made that clicking sound again, getting Janey and Cobb to lope into a faster trot despite our heavy load. "I think we'd better get to Ma. You two keep an eye out while I take us home."

Pa urged the team across the last few miles until the trail took us down to the mud at the edge of our crick. I heard my dog barking somewhere near the house, still out of sight. There was a pistol shot before we crossed. And the shout of a man's voice filled with fury.

Then I heard Ma scream.

CHAPTER 2

MY HEART POUNDED at the sound of her voice. "Hup, hup!" growled Pa, lurching the mules into the water, trundling our wagon onward.

"Miss Mae, get your head down!" said Mister Coates.

Ma cried out again, making me angry, afraid we weren't moving fast enough. But I did as Mister Coates told me, shifted my form lower, watching him hold that shotgun tight in his fists while Janey and Cobb clamored out of the crick at the far side. Pa pushed them hard through the cottonwoods and started across the lower pasture.

The farm came into view, and we saw two horses tied to the posts by the front porch. A third stood at the gate to the barn. No riders in sight. My dog was between us and them, lying motionless in the grass. The door to the house was open.

I shifted on my knees, trying to understand what I saw. The weight of what I was witnessing not yet clear in my mind.

Pa drove the team closer.

"God be with us, Mister Kepler. This is not looking good," said Mister Coates.

That's when I felt something warm and wet splash across my face. I heard the crack of a rifle and realized Pa was tumbling back on top of me. I think Mister Coates grabbed the reins because the wagon slowed. Before it came to a stop there was another rifle shot. Mister Coates grunted and tried to say something before he fell off the side of the buckboard onto the ground beside us.

The weight of my pa slammed into me, pressed me between bins and bundles and against the floor of the wagon bed. He weren't moving and I feared he was hurt bad. It took me a few tries to remove myself from under him.

"Pa?" I said right away, pushing at his shoulder to get him to get back up. His eyes looking at me but not seeing. "Mister Coates!" I said, just as quick. "Help me with Pa."

But there was no answer.

I tried to wipe the blood covering the side of Pa's face. It was warm and slick and there was so much. The red began to saturate the shoulder of his coat when I realized the breath of life no longer came from Pa's mouth or nose.

I became afraid.

Felt abandoned and I began to cry. Holding my daddy in my arms, not knowing what else to do. Feeling his warmth still coming from his form and not wanting to let that last bit of him leave me — seep away as my own anger rose inside.

Then I heard a horse coming. I pulled away from Pa and saw the big man with the ginger beard ride close, pointing his rifle at me.

"You slain my pa," I said, trying to push away my fears. I wiped the tears from my cheeks with the back of a bloodied hand, feeling a burning hate fill my heart.

The rider dismounted and I realized he was fixing to grab me. "Don't you touch me, you murdering bastard."

I stood in the wagon bed, but had nowhere to go, and this feller turned out to be bigger up close than I'd supposed — even off his stout quarter horse. He had broad shoulders and was a tower of a man. His long, sharp, Mexican-style spurs jingled with each step.

Without pause, he spun that rifle in his hands, swung it, and clubbed me to fall against the provisions piled behind me. I tried to rise back up to fight, but my head spun. I didn't have a chance to shout or anything before the brute struck again, hitting my chin, knocking me back on my bum.

I pushed at his hands and face when he climbed in to gag me with a kerchief. Squirmed until he pulled a length of rope from his belt and pushed his body against mine. Him hog-tying my wrists and ankles together like a pig for slaughter. Once done, I could only watch as he patted the pockets of Pa's coat with his hands until he found the box with the locket and a small bag of coin.

The big man jumped back down to the ground, and I heard him kick Mister Coates, I guess to see if he was alive or dead. Then the sound of them spurs wandered away as he led his horse the rest of the distance to the house. Left me there in the back of the wagon with Pa. Fearing for my ma. Worried they'd do to her what they'd already done to the only other two people I truly knew and loved in the world.

CHAPTER 3

I DON'T KNOW how long I lay, but I stirred when I heard Ma. The house was not far, so I could hear them men too as they laughed and cajoled one another while they were doing God knows what to her. Something broke and glass shattered. Ma spoke with pain in her voice. I couldn't tell what she said and couldn't call to her on account of the kerchief.

I wanted to scream.

Ma started sobbing. She shouted my name clear as day. There was a pistol shot, and then everything was quiet. My fears returned as did the tears in my eyes. I felt like I was sinking into some deep black well. Like I was drowning in dark waters.

There was silence for a time, until Janey shifted her weight and moved the wagon a foot or two. Cobb snapped at her for being such an impatient mule. My mind surfaced and I heard the four voices again.

"The girl is in the wagon. You finish her, boy, while me and these two fools gather the animals in the barn."

"Speak for yerself, Little John," said the feller with the squeaky voice.

"Yeah, speak for yerself," echoed the third.

"Shut up and get those animals. Got no time to bicker," the

11

big man told them. There was a shuffling of boots on wood. I heard footsteps cross the mud in the yard to the barn.

"What about me, sir? What should I do… with that girl… and her mama?" the boy asked.

"Whatever you like, Boy. Just make sure they ain't breathing when you're spent. Bring the two mules and meet us to the north at Jacob's Ferry by sundown."

I heard the big man mount his quarter horse and ride to join the others at the barn. I didn't hear the boy, so I figured he was still in the house. The three men started yipping. Making the sounds drovers make when they round cattle to move. As the big man ushered them to go, I heard his now familiar voice boom out across our yard at the boy. "Why are you still standing there in the door? Finish what I told you."

The boy stepped off the porch, the sound of his feet crunching in the loose stone by our front step. "I will," he promised.

"Well, get on with it. This day will be done before you know. And we got more of these sodbusters to call on tomorrow."

There was silence for a time. Pa's form was still close against me as I waited for that boy to do as he was told and cross the distance from the farmhouse to the wagon. When his footfalls did draw near, I heard him gulp in some air, breathing short and rapid. His young face appeared above the broad sideboard. The boy's fingers curled over the edge to hold on. They were red and chapped; his nails chewed down to the nub. He acted surprised when he saw me there all tied up.

I glared and fidgeted, pulling at the rope on my wrists.

He stared, like he was deciding something. Then spoke: "Little John was right. You ain't very pretty."

I balled my fists, wishing to poke him in the eye as his right hand disappeared and returned holding a big Jim Bowie knife.

The boy clamored up onto the back wheel of the wagon to join me in the bed. My entire body grew tight, figuring he'd start with something worse before moving on to the killing part. Until, that is, Mister Coates silently appeared like Abaddon, the angel of death, wrapped an arm around the boy and stuck an even bigger knife in the side of his throat. The boy's eyes grew wide before Mister Coates let him fall back into the cold, wet grass. He wasted no time climbing in to cut away my binds.

"You alright, Miss Mae?"

I must have blinked, fluttering my eyes in disbelief. I heard the boy gurgle and choke before he went still. Mister Coates took my hands between his and squeezed, pulling me back from the depths of all that sudden violence and loss. The weight of my fear lifted as he removed the kerchief stuffed against my mouth and used it to wipe the blood from the gash on my chin.

In that moment, I hugged him with all the love I had left inside of me.

Mister Coates was wounded but seemed like he didn't care. After checking Pa, he picked up the shotgun still in the grass, and led me quickly to the house where we found Ma inside; her dress torn. Her body curled and exposed on the floor beneath our supper table. A broken water pitcher and dishes were scattered about her.

Those men had done bad things. There was blood coming from her private places and she'd been shot through the back.

But Ma was still breathing.

Relief filled my heart, and the fear I'd felt before rose again. My mind raced, losing all sense of what should be done.

Without me asking, Mister Coates got a blanket to cover her dignity, and we moved close, each taking one of Ma's hands. She stirred and coughed but did not open her eyes and would not speak.

"Ma, I'm here... and I love you," I whispered, pressing closer. Not wanting to lose her too. I brushed the tangled, brown hair from her eyes and smelled the gunpowder that still lingered inside our home.

Mister Coates touched my shoulder. "Miss Mae, I... I believe you've got to go. Those men might come back when that boy doesn't show."

I held Ma a moment more, hearing Mister Coates' words, but not wanting to leave my ma's side. Me hanging on to the rise and fall of each breath. Listening to the beat of her heart.

I finally kissed Ma on the cheek and told her she was the strongest woman I knew.

"You'll be alright?" I said to Mister Coates when I pulled away.

"I'll survive, God willing. Long as you find us some help from town."

I looked at him a moment – at his familiar dark face and deep brown eyes. "You saved me, Mister Coates," I said, and he took my hands in his again, replying with only a tight smile.

"What about Pa?" I worried on and he spoke, struggling to keep the thickness of his own sorrow inside.

"I'll make him a proper grave and mark it too."

I felt my lips quiver and the tears returned. "Maybe by the crick... beneath the cottonwoods?"

Mister Coates nodded. "Unhitch Janey and take that boy's pistol. I know he got one under his blanket. I'll nurse your Ma and keep those men from getting back in here best as I can until you send Doc and the law."

I didn't want to leave but knew Mister Coates was right. Both their lives now depended upon my getting to town as quick as I could.

CHAPTER 4

MY JAW ACHED something terrible as I grabbed another blanket, filling it with some of the biscuits Ma had made that morning. Some taters and onions too. I figured my run for the doctor in Weld might turn into a night under the stars, so I rolled everything inside a rain slicker. Mister Coates moved Ma to her bed, pulling the quilts up around her to keep her warm. He brought wood in from the porch to boil a kettle while I traded my skirt for Ma's buckskin riding pants and yanked on my boots.

Ma moaned in pain, so I came to her side again. Kissed her on her forehead and turned to Mister Coates, giving him another hug. "The doc will come. The sheriff too, I promise."

"You be careful, Miss Mae," Mister Coates said. "Those butchers are out there."

I took Pa's ragged Slouch hat and work coat from the pegs by the door and ran to get that pistol and unhitch Janey. Course I'd already wasted enough time and wanted to go straight for the wagon, but when I saw my dog, I had to stop. I knelt beside him and rested my hand on his shaggy flank to say goodbye. His body was already cold. Chilled by the damp breeze. Them men shot him through the side of his head, so I knew he did not suffer. My pa neither.

I felt hate pump back inside my heart and I looked up at the evening sky, vowing to kill these men. If I couldn't hire

15

somebody to do it, I'd find them one by one, and do it myself. And when it was done, I'd come back to Ma, Mister Coates, and our farm.

The pistol was right where Mister Coates said I'd find it. I couldn't gaze upon the boy's face, but I knelt and slipped the gun out of the waist of his trousers. The pistol was heavy and dull. It was old and hadn't been cared for very well. But it had a full load of cap and ball.

And it was all I had.

I stood again, not looking at Pa, not wanting to remember him in such a way. Silent and broken and twisted. Both of the mules eyed me, giving me a quizzical glare as I unhitched Janey. Cobb hawed with an uneasiness, somehow knowing I was going to leave him. He watched as I led Janey to the barn.

The broad doors were open, and all the animals gone. Six steers, two calves, a donkey, and our milking cow. They'd taken Pa's white-booted sorrel too.

How he loved that horse.

I set a saddle on Janey and laced two leather bags against it to hang across her rump. Put the slicker and food in one and part of a sack of feed for her in the other and grabbed two canteens to fill with water later. Then I remembered Pa's trouble money. I didn't know how long it was gonna take to find those men. God and the devil knew I'd need some currency for the job, and I found it where Pa kept it hidden – wedged low in a dark, dry place at the back of Janey and Cobb's stall. One hundred-thirty US dollars in a mason jar saved a few bills at a time for what Pa always said would be "that which arrives unannounced."

Shoving the greenbacks into the left pocket of his coat, I felt for the pistol deep in the other. I placed one foot in a stirrup, mounted Janey and rode to get help.

In a flurry I passed through the cottonwoods, the crick, and beyond to the prairie as the sky darkened. Went a mile and more along the narrow track to Weld before easing a little for old Janey. We trotted a few dozen yards so she could catch her wind again until I felt a queer sense someone was watching us.

Alone with only Janey and on vacant land, I thought of them killers again, fearing the three had returned to retrieve that boy. I reined the mule to stop in the faded light and looked all about. My hand found the pistol again deep in Pa's coat pocket, pulling it when I heard the crack of a dry branch snap. I swung the gun towards the sound. Cocked back the hammer with my thumb and aimed at a tangle of scrub not twenty feet away.

"I... I know you're there," I said, hearing my own voice waver. "Come on out."

The dim prairie went silent all about me.

The branches parted and I found myself gazing upon another set of eyes peering back. A sad face pushed out, adorned on top with a pair of long, droopy ears.

Feller weren't no murdering thief or part of an outlaw gang; it was Robert, our stolen donkey.

He came the rest of the way through the bramble blowing air through his lips and crooked teeth when he realized who I was. Maybe it was a foolish thing, but I dismounted and threw my arms about Robert's neck. He nudged me, swished his funny little tail, kissing and licking my face.

"Always the brute," I whispered, still hugging him.

Robert had somehow broken free from the other animals Little John's rabble had taken. A frayed lead hung from his harness and dragged on the ground. The hurt of losing my pa, and the wounds Ma and Mister Coates suffered – the pain of all these returned as the familiar donkey nuzzled under my arm.

Not wanting him to become lost again and with no time to return a donkey to our barn, I decided to bring Robert along too. I tied his line to Janey's rig and the three of us ran on, the rest of the way to town, fast as we could again, watching a distant storm churn way to the south as we went. The squall's flashes of lighting flickered across the horizon, giving the dark prairie an eerie glow.

Night had truly arrived by the time we came into Weld. Janey seemed happy she was wearing a saddle instead of her having to pull that heavy buckboard through the muddy street. Robert's donkey ears were high, him revealing his own excitement from being with familiar friends again — unaware of the bloody turn the day had taken.

Despite the possibility of danger, I chose to drive Janey straight down Main, wagering them three outlaws would be waiting for the boy miles to the north at Jacob's Ferry. The street was empty, but there was piano music and laughter coming out of the saloon down the way. The mercantile was dark. Livery and land office too. I tied the animals to one of the hitches in front of the barbershop and prayed to Jesus Ma was still alive as I climbed the stairs up the back to Doc Lowry's place.

He was there, appearing like an answer to a prayer after I knocked.

"Mae Kepler?" Lowry said, squinting at me around his half-open door, shining light across my form from a bullseye lantern he held in one hand. Doc gazed about to see if anyone was with me or was watching before motioning at me to come inside.

His apartment was simple and smelled like pipe tobacco and charcoal. He had a lot of books on shelves. A bed, two chairs and a small round table next to a little box stove that was glowing. "I almost thought you were your daddy. You in that hat and coat."

"There's no time," I said when Doc wanted me to sit. "Pa's dead, and Ma hurt bad. Mister Coates too. They were all shot."

"Shot?"

"Three men and a boy done it."

He motioned again for me to use one of the chairs and I shook my head.

"I don't want to sit. Ma might be dying. I... I need you to ride... tend to her and Mister Coates." I began to cry right then, and Doc Lowry made me sit anyway. The warmth of the embers radiated out of the stove and felt good, melting away the chill from my ride.

"You know this for sure?"

"Course I know it... I was there. I'd be dead too if it weren't for Mister Coates. Those murderers took our livestock. All of the cattle and Pa's horse. Left that boy to finish me and Ma, but Mister Coates had other ideas."

"Your face, Miss Mae," Doc Lowry said after I'd finished, noticing the wound on my chin.

"It don't matter," I told him. "You've got to go, Doc." But he brushed my insistence aside and cleaned it anyway with some foul, yellowy liquid. Wanted to use a bandage until I stood.

"Stop your fussing," I said. "There is no time. I only came to get you. Send you back home to help Ma. I don't know if she'll make it through this night."

He quick placed the medicine back in his bag and buckled it closed. "Do you know their names? Who they were?"

I shook my head again, pulling Doc to his feet to get him going. Feeling overwhelmed, worried he was moving too slow. "They called the big one, Little John," I said as Lowry got his coat. "He... he was good with one of them short Spencer rifles. Doc, we didn't do anything to them. They got there before we made it back from the mercantile. Shot my dog. Then Pa and Mister Coates. Had unnatural relations with Ma, I'm pretty sure."

He swallowed. Put on his hat, still thinking on my words. "You said *send me back*. Where are you planning to go, Miss Mae?"

"To find Sheriff Conley."

Doc looked skeptical like I was sharing a bad proposition. "I expect he's at Hancock's," Doc said, locking his door, me hustling him down his steps. "The sheriff usually enjoys a beer or two first part of the evening."

I ushered him across to the livery with Janey and Robert in tow. Helped Doc retrieve his mount in earnest. "Are you sure you don't want me to go with you before I ride? I mean, to help explain all this," he said, peering down at me from his saddle.

"It'll be a simple conversation. Sheriff knows us from church."

I smacked the horse's rump and Doc galloped into the dark, east towards our farm, coaxing that horse hard - me not knowing if he'd be quick enough to save Ma.

"Hurry!" I shouted after him before he was gone. "Make sure you tell Mister Coates who's knocking. He's got Pa's shotgun."

CHAPTER 5

THE MERCANTILE HAD a small counter for beer and whiskey and some accommodations for rent above, but Hancock's was the real saloon in town. I'd heard the stories. How four whores kept rooms in back and that men could take a hot bath for a dime. Up front was said to be more elegant, with a piano and a bar and a row of stools. Tables for cards. The owner served liquor, beer and tobacco and offered a plate of something with a piece of bread and a cup of strong coffee.

I moved Janey and Robert and tied them opposite where there was an open hitch rack across the street. My boots sloshed through the muck as I crossed back to where I stomped and scraped them on the wooden steps below the saloon entrance. There I witnessed my reflection for the first time since Pa's murder. My dignity sinking like a stone in a pond as I gazed at myself in the pane of glass set in one of the doors. A soiled face and battered chin showed beneath Pa's old hat. And the coat I wore was so large and rumpled I might as well have been a fifteen-year-old boy standing there.

Little John and his cohorts had been nothing but right. There wasn't much pretty about the girl who stared back at me from the glass. And there was no improvement to speak of when I turned up the cuffs on Pa's coat to try and make it all look a little better. I remembered Ma again and climbed them steps to get on

20

with why I come.

Pa liked to puff on a cigar now and again. And I'd seen him drink beer at weddings and maybe once take a sip of rye. But truth be told, I'd never been to a saloon like Hancock's before until I pushed my way inside.

Within, smoke hung in the air and the chatter of conversation filled the space. The front room wasn't all that grand. Lesser than the picture I'd painted of it in my mind.

Through the haze one of them whores was standing at the bar with three cowboys giggling like she knew something they didn't. More men sat at tables, smoking, drinking, playing cards. A piano player plunked out something that sounded a whole lot livelier than the music we sang in church vespers. And even though I was only fifteen, no one seemed to care I'd arrived, so I moved quickly to the bar where the owner stood wiping a glass with a damp cloth.

"Mister Hancock, you seen the sheriff?"

He looked at me funny for a moment after I spoke, not replying in any way. I figured I didn't ask loud enough, with the noise and all. "The sheriff, have you seen him?" I said again.

Hancock leaned forward. "Mae Kepler, is that you?" He took in the hat and coat I was wearing, obviously a little bewildered. "Ain't it late for you to be in town? Your daddy is going to be angry; he finds out you've been in here."

"Pa's shot-dead, Mister Hancock. I need to speak to the sheriff if you know where he is."

"Dead?"

His eyes darted to a corner of the room, and I saw Sheriff Conley sitting with a younger feller at one of the tables. Each with a half empty glass of beer.

"Thank you kindly, Mister Hancock," I said, and spun on my heels to head towards the man I was looking for. The walk across that noisy establishment made my heart beat fast again. I saw Pa and Ma and Mister Coates, repeating in my mind's eye what three men had done to them hours before.

Conley was older with gray in his large mustache and at his temples. He was a widower whose wife had died of fever a year before. I didn't know the young one beside him. Sheriff slid his

21

hat back off his brow with a thumb when he saw me coming, whispered to the boy before taking a sip as I drew close.

The young feller looked at me with curiosity and touched the brim of his. "Ma'am."

Before I could open my mouth, I realized the sheriff knew who I was. "Miss Kepler. What the hell are you wearing and what did you do to your chin?"

Made me feel like a little kid.

I sat and tried to say the same story I'd just recited to Doc Lowry, but before I could get three words out tears started spilling from my eyes. I heard the rifle and recalled Pa's body landing on mine again. Saw Ma curled under our table bloody and violated and with a pistol wound in her back.

The sheriff squirmed, facing me with my tears and wringing hands. "Go easy, Mae," he whispered. "Say what you must slow and true."

Sheriff Conley and his wife had never been blessed with a child of their own, but he was patient enough as I unspooled once again what I'd been a part of only hours before.

"This here's Lucas Barrientos," Sheriff said with a nod at the boy when I finished the telling and took a breath. "Luke's my new deputy."

I wiped some of the tears from my face. "Nice to meet you." The feller was slight and had big ears. The bangs of his dark hair fell into his eyes, which were wide open. He looked a little spooked after hearing my story but offered me a warm smile.

The sheriff motioned at Mister Hancock. Got him to pour me a small glass of beer. I suppose he thought that might calm me down. Hancock didn't linger. He backed away and returned to his counter and the sheriff placed one of his hands over mine. "God bless you child," he whispered.

In him I saw genuine anguish behind his weary eyes. He glanced at the young feller beside him before leaning closer to me. "I knew your Pa pretty well. He was a good sort. Your place falls beyond my line of authority, but as a favor, Luke and I will ride out there in the morning. Can't follow those killers, though, Miss Kepler, on account of my jurisdiction. I am not the law in the Colorado Territory. Folks here hired me for the town. That's all. You'll need to seek a marshal for hunting fugitives."

I didn't know what to say, me not really knowing much about the law and all. My mind ran like a jack rabbit, full of worry about Ma and Mister Coates. Fortunately, the sheriff didn't leave me hanging long and offered a ray of hope. "There is a fellow who I believe is a federal marshal staying at Mrs. Johnson's. Least he was there this morning. Perhaps he could help with your situation."

Deputy Luke and the sheriff escorted me outside back into the night. Luke wished me well, taking my hand in his before he left.

"He's an honest kid," the sheriff remarked, him doing his best to keep up with me as I scurried towards the western edge of town. "Luke's parents live down in the New Mexico Territory. Good people. That boy will make a fine officer of the peace someday."

Sheriff Conley's conversation had run its course by the time we arrived in front of the big home situated at the end of Main Street. He and I gazed at Mrs. Johnson's Boarding House through the dim light, which loomed long, with a broad porch and a second story. Beyond it, I saw the prairie that stretched far into the distance towards the Rocky Mountains.

The sheriff knocked on the fancy door that had an etched pane set within it. Mrs. Johnson appeared with a glowing hurricane lamp, offering us to enter, and me busting past her into her foyer without allowing the sheriff a moment to explain why we'd come so late.

"I must speak with the marshal," I said before realizing how fancy the room was I stood in. "I... I'm desperate for his help."

Mrs. Johnson looked confused, first gazing upon me by the light of her lamp, then turning to Conley. "Sheriff?"

He removed his hat. "Ma'am."

She turned again to me.

"I am sorry, Mrs. Johnson, ma'am," I said. "I know it's rude and that you probably don't know me."

I extended my hand.

"I'm Mae Kepler, ma'am. Is he here... the US marshal, I mean? May I speak with him?"

Mrs. Johnson took a breath. Looked at Conley again. "There is a man here who wears the badge of a marshal. But he's long gone to his bed after drinking a half bottle of Rye."

"You'll not wake him?" I said, thinking only of Ma and Pa and them killers. The sheriff took my hand, holding it against his hip as if to rein me in.

Then he took a breath, apologized for both of us again and explained my situation.

"You poor thing," said Mrs. Johnson. She gave me a hug but was steadfast when it came to waking her customers — especially one as prominent as a US marshal. She said her brother would picket Janey and Robert out back. And that for thirty-five cents she'd feed me and put me up for the night with some quilts on the floor in her small parlor. "Miss Kepler, I promise you can speak with the marshal in the morning," she said.

Course I weren't pleased.

The sheriff left me with Mrs. Johnson for the night, and I tossed and turned. What sleep came to me was full of rotten dreams and not much peace. When I rose with the crows, all I could think on was how I was going to convince a federal lawman to drop everything and help me track Pa's killers.

I folded them quilts in a neat pile, and I went out back to relieve myself and check on my mule and the donkey. I took Pa's hat but left the coat inside. It was cold like it had been the morning before on the ride to town with Pa and Mister Coates.

Janey hawed when she saw me, saying she was hungry, so I pulled some dry hay for her from Mrs. Johnson's shed. Robert flicked his tail; happy I'd come to join them. He was nibbling on frosty bits of grass. As the sky began to brighten, I shivered, wishing I'd worn that coat. But before I could retrieve it, I heard a set of boots descend Mrs. Johnson's back step.

I turned to find a man standing there looking at me and Janey. He was wearing a gray wool long coat with broad lapels. His dark hair was long enough to tickle his shoulders, but it was matted, like he'd just woken up. The feller was of average height and clean-shaven. Handsome, despite his unkept appearance.

"I don't have no comb, if that's what you're looking for," I said.

He raised his arms to touch his hair, running his fingers through it to mash it back in place. I figured he was maybe ten years older than me.

"Better?" he said as if seeking redemption.

I felt embarrassed for being smart mouthed with him. And expect he didn't notice my cheeks turning a little shade of crimson in the early morning light.

"That what you're riding?"

"Janey's a good mule," I replied. "And that's my ass." I gestured with a nod and took a few steps towards Robert, leaning in to scratch his mane. When I turned back, the feller weren't looking at my face.

"Backside's a little flat, but it looks sturdy enough."

His gaze made me uneasy. "Mister, I'm in no mood for any man's affection, if that is what's on your mind."

"Making an observation."

"Well, I'm only fifteen you should know. Haven't even had breakfast yet."

"Course not. Guess you're not quite a woman, are you? And I ain't no mister. You best call me Marshal." He lifted his coat lapel to reveal a silver star pinned to the shirt he wore beneath and quickly redirected our line of conversation. "What's the burro's name?"

I told him and scratched Robert beneath his chin, realizing this was the man I'd worried and waited all night to speak with. The marshal stepped closer, eyeing me again.

I knew I should remain polite and smile but couldn't at first, thinking of Ma and Pa, and how much my life had changed from one cold morning to the very next. Until I remembered it was my daddy who'd given Robert his name.

"I suppose it is a little queer for a donkey to be called that. My pa weren't no friend of the Confederacy. Didn't much care for Robert E. Lee neither. Said he was a jackass for signing up on the wrong side."

"Matter of opinion, I suppose."

"Got nothing to do with opinion. This here Robert is the finest ass."

The marshal laughed at that, looking me up and down again.

"What about yours?" he continued without pause. "Your name, I mean."

My disquiet returned, me knowing I did not want any such attention. Not then. All I needed was this man's skill and station to hunt the three men I sought.

Course I grew flushed despite these facts. And the marshal noticed this time, for the sun had peaked above the corner of Mrs. Johnson's shed.

"Mae," I said, forcing myself to look him straight in the eye. "Mae Kepler."

CHAPTER 6

HARRY STURGES WAS his name, and he told me he was indeed a United States Deputy Marshal. Newly minted. Said taming the Colorado Territory was his first assignment. He'd been too young to serve in the war, tried to study some Law back east in Virginia, but a desk weren't no place for him.

I interrupted his tale to explain my predicament while Mrs. Johnson fed us an early breakfast. The marshal helped me carry my things out to Janey and Robert.

"I'm supposed to meet a solicitor in Ogallala, Nebraska six days forward," he said. "Being that your fugitives stole some cattle, that might be where they're headed. Although it's the tail end of the season for driving, they may have stashed a mixed herd north near the Platte."

We lifted my saddle on Janey, and he helped me strap the cinch and billets to make them tight. "You think they're going to ship them on the railroad?" I asked.

"No. I think the plan is to sell them. Let some other fool handle the shipment."

"Will you help me, Marshal Sturges?"

He looked me up and down again. Took his broad, dark hat off and made like he was adjusting the leather band that ran

27

above its brim. "You'll have to pay my fee."

"Fee? Exactly what kind of fee are you aiming to get? My pa always paid his share at the land office proper. Don't all them taxes cover your pay?"

He scowled and put his hat back on his head. "I don't mean nothing inappropriate ma'am. We marshals don't draw wages, you know. Everything is based on a fee, or a reward set by the court. Being that there's no judge involved yet, I think a contracted fee is the appropriate measure in this particular situation. You think on it while I recover my belongings and saddle my horse."

As he strode off in his long coat, I noticed that young deputy-feller Luke riding towards me. He tipped his hat. His appearance seemed better in the light of day - not so short up there on a horse. His ears were still sticking out, though.

"You really going with that man alone?" said Luke, eyeing Harry Sturges as he walked off.

"He's a marshal, ain't he? The law says I need a marshal to get those men that killed my pa."

"There's no one here who can vouch for his nature," Luke said right back. His eyes kept watching Sturges amble down the street and disappear into the local livery yard before he turned his gaze on me again.

"What, you offering your expertise, Deputy? Worried he might take advantage?" I double-tied Robert's lead to Janey. "I can take care of myself."

"I expect maybe you can," Luke said with an uneasy smile. He shifted in his saddle, looking back up the street. "Sheriff Conley would be upset if I disappeared without notice, anyway."

"Well, you best get on with your day. I've got plenty to think about and to do without wasting time standing here gabbing with you."

The boy tipped his hat again and I watched him trot away and peek into the stable where the marshal had gone before moving on towards the sheriff's office.

I knew I needed to trail them killers without further delay, but I had no idea what I should offer Marshal Sturges. It wasn't like there was another federal lawman nearby to allow me to haggle on a price. How was I supposed to know a rate fair for hiring a gun good enough to chase down three murdering fugitives? I thought of Pa, feeling the pain of his death again. Knowing he'd have an answer for what to do. Lord, the only money I had anyway was from his mason jar.

I decided I'd offer thirty dollars to start. I figured if we found this feller Little John and his co-conspirators, I could offer the marshal Pa's sorrel as a concluding payment. Assuming we found the horse. I prayed it would be enough.

Sturges returned riding a dapple gray. The horse was tall - at least 17 hands, and his eyes were as black as the wide-brimmed hat the marshal wore. There was a Winchester in a buckskin scabbard slung from the right side of his saddle. A bedroll and twin satchels were laced across the gelding's rump.

The sun had risen, pushing the clouds away, leaving only blue above us. Sturges opened his long coat in the warmer air, letting it fall behind a twin pistol rig he wore at his hips.

"Looks like I'm getting my money's worth."

"Exactly how much is that?" he said, reminding me we hadn't yet come to terms.

In short order, we settled on forty dollars to start. I paid him in greenbacks and, again, wasn't happy. But Sturges promised the sorrel would do in the end to finish what I owed - if we ever recovered him. If not, the marshal agreed another forty would close our contract.

On the way out of town we stopped at Crenshaw's Mercantile. The owner and his wife came to me as soon as we entered to offer their condolences. Word had already spread about the murder of my pa. "We were just visiting and joking not a day ago," he said. His wife gave me a hug and they both reassured me our tab was in good standing. "Your folks never failed to remit a debt owed."

Course, I thanked them for their kindness, and, so not to lose any more time, let the wife help me find what I needed. I used credit to buy another blanket, wool socks, *Arbuckle's* coffee, two tins of crackers, a wedge of cheese, hard candy, and a small sack of apples. The marshal didn't have anything to cook in, so I also purchased a decent-sized skillet and a kettle to boil the coffee in.

"You sure you don't need anything else, Mae Kepler?" Sturges asked, looking at all the merchandise I'd gathered. I signed the bill and waited while he bought cartridges for his Winchester '66, some chaw tobacco, jerky, and a bottle of Rye. Then we rode for Jacob's Ferry.

Least that was the plan. But we didn't get that far.

Young Luke reappeared at the edge of town, sitting on a different horse. His outfit was better too – a brown hat, scarf, and a clean Mackinaw long coat that all looked nice against the color of his russet-brown bay. His city deputy badge was pinned to the breast of the coat. A single revolver was holstered and tied to the horn of his saddle.

"We met the other day," remarked the marshal. "Everything alright?"

Luke acknowledged Sturges and turned to me. I decided not to mention to the marshal about him stopping to check on me earlier, so I only smiled. "The sheriff was worried, Miss Mae. Said it was unwise for one lawman to take on the men who killed your Pa."

"Conley said that?" Sturges said.

Luke nodded in his direction. "Yes sir. No offense meant, sir."

"None taken. I suppose you're the man to fill the slot?" the marshal replied with a glance at me. I figured I'd better say something.

"Coming to rescue me, are you? Does the sheriff know you're here?" I wanted to see if he'd done what he said he wouldn't do.

Luke blushed. "He won't be happy, but I did leave him a note. Last night he said nice things about your pa. If it were mine somebody done this crime to, I'd pray for as much help as I could get."

Marshal Sturges spoke again: "We need to ride, but I could use another gun if you know how to use it. You ever apprehend a fugitive before?"

"Mostly drunk cowpokes. Nothing like a murderer or anything, but I am good with a pistol, and will do what you say, Marshal, sir."

"Should take a few days. Don't want you to lose your job or

nothing."

Luke shrugged. "I don't think it'll come to that, sir. My leaving to help a woman in need... I can't believe such a thing would hurt my standing with Sheriff Conley." Luke gave me a nervous eye as he said it.

"Well, alright then," agreed Sturges, cutting his horse closer alongside Luke's bay. "I'll federalize your authority. But your cut comes from Miss Kepler directly, not out of my fee. We clear?"

"Yes sir. If that's okay with you Miss Mae?"

"Just what I need: two deputies." Course, I knew bringing along another lawman was prudent. Even if it was this boy with the big ears. Luke grinned when I offered him twenty dollars and a share of our food and supplies. Payment would take place once Little John and his associates were dead or apprehended.

"I'm done wasting time with all these discussions," I finally announced to both. "My pa's killers are out there... getting farther away with each passing hour. It's time to get on with this deed."

The marshal's eyes grew steely. "Well, boy, if you know the way, why don't you lead Miss Kepler and me north to the ferry?"

"Yes, sir!" said Luke with a fresh dose of delight. "Ma'am," he added with a tip of his hat at me and got his bay to trotting. That russet-brown horse's black mane and tail fluttered with each step. "Two hours and not much more," Luke promised over his shoulder, still grinning about the knowledge that the marshal had agreed to include him in our little enterprise. I followed, riding Janey, and leading my donkey, Robert. Marshal Harry Sturges took to the rear.

CHAPTER 7

JANEY KEPT HER distance from Luke and his bay, no matter how much I tried to coax the mule to speed up and lose the extra ground between us. I glanced behind at the marshal who was still following some ten yards back. Suppose he was amused by my predicament.

"I don't think Janey likes your horse," I called after Luke. "She won't go no faster."

"Maybe I can fix that," said the boy.

He pulled something out of one of his saddlebags and turned about, holding his reins in one hand, displaying a plump, white turnip in the other. Janey's ears perked when she eyed that root, sniffing, and changed her mind all of a sudden to get closer. She bolted forward, dragging me and Robert with her, wasting no time to make the turnip disappear with a crunch of delight. Luke gave one to Robert too and the both of them animals stuck fast to the young deputy and his handsome bay forever after.

Course that's when I discovered the boy's true nature.

Turned out Lucas Barrientos was a real chatterbox. Ready and willing to share all sorts of facts about almost anything. He pulled his horse beside me, Janey and Robert. Started by explaining how far it was to the Nebraska border north of the river. Told me about the Indians who used to live along the Platte, east across the plains, and got excited when he spoke of the steam engines we might observe if we made it all the way to Ogallala. Luke sowed plenty of words, but it was a good way to pass the time. I noticed even the marshal kept his horse in a little tighter behind me when Luke was speaking. He wanted to enjoy all them stories and facts as well.

I'd only crossed the ferry once to look at livestock with Ma and Pa up north. It'd been early Spring, and the flowers were peeking up through the soft, green prairie. Butterflies and birds were in abundance. Now the grass was stiff and dormant and colorless. But at least the sun was shining. The open ground kept spreading out before us. The trail dropped down through each dip and reappeared again after each rise. Following a straight course across the land until finally, in the distance, we spotted a line of trees running roughly west to east.

"That's the river," Luke said with certainty. "Jacob's Ferry is in the woods, and as I recall, there's a small general store on the far side."

He pulled ahead of me, and I slowed to wait for the marshal to catch up. Robert sniffed at the lawman's big dapple. His donkey-ears drooped, letting me know he wasn't sure if he liked that gelding quite yet. Janey matched the horse's speed, dragging my Robert along whether he wanted to come or not.

"Both your animals seem to be prickly about making new acquaintances," Sturges remarked, pulling along side of me.

"Maybe they're just being protective?"

The marshal took me in again with his eyes like he always seemed to be doing. Making me feel uneasy about him again. "It is a bold thing, Miss Kepler," he said. "Riding alone with two men you barely know out in open country such as this."

Robert tugged again on his lead, distracting me for a moment. Being ornery as only donkeys can be. After I scolded him and got him back in line again, I turned back toward Sturges.

"Well, my pa is dead, and my ma's been shot. Violated. The only thing left is to make it right. Find the men that done it."

When he remained silent, I let Janey trot on a short distance before speaking again, wanting to change the direction of our conversation. "So, you been here before?" I asked, the marshal's horse keeping pace beside me as we rode the last mile to the river.

Sturges spit out a wad of tobacco juice. "Don't think so."

"What do you mean? You either been here or not. I've crossed here twice. Once going north. Once going south when I was eleven."

"I'm happy you are so certain about everything, Mae Kepler. This Colorado Territory all looks the same. It's not like my home of Virginia. This place has more grass than trees, and the roads are nothing but mud and shit."

"Virginia don't have no horse shit?"

"Course we do, Virginians pay folks to clean it up before too long. Citizens back east are what you call *organized*."

"Organized or not, the mud will be gone soon," I reassured him. "Once the ground freezes."

"You're almost as bad as Luke. Full of pleasant facts I'll be sure to remember."

Sturges kicked his spurs into the flank of his dapple and rode forward to catch up with his new subordinate. I watched the two of them speak. The marshal made the boy laugh, probably at my expense, because Luke peered back and waved with another big grin on his face. They kept chatting as I rode Janey and led Robert after them.

Soon enough, Luke passed Sturges his pistol - I guess to show him. The older man held it in the grip of his hand, feeling its weight and balance. He aimed it at the horizon, then swung his arm to point the barrel of the gun at Luke with a stern expression on his face. The marshal cocked the hammer back and I thought my heart would stop beating, fearing his handsome smile had truly tricked my sensibilities.

That boy about turned to stone, the way his face went all ashen. Sturges laughed, re-secured the hammer, and let the pistol roll forward on his finger before handing it back to Luke butt-first. "Don't give a man your weapon," I heard the marshal say. "Especially if you don't really know him. Might be the last bad decision you choose to make."

Luke turned back to see if I was watching, which of course I was. His eyes revealed his embarrassment and more than a little shame as he placed the revolver back in its holster.

Jacob's Ferry hadn't changed much. A flat barge made from

timber was lashed to a hemp cable strung up and across the South Platte. The forest Luke had spoken of wasn't much. It was made from a narrow line of dormant hardwood. The road cut through these before ending at the rock-strewn bank of the river.

There was indeed a small structure on the far side, as Luke had recalled. A hand-painted sign read "Dry Goods & Café." The café part sounded fancy, and I had no recollection of it from the last time I'd crossed with my parents. Luke and the marshal held their horses and waited for me to catch up to them.

"Let me go first to speak with the ferryman so I can negotiate a price," said the marshal. "I don't want him to overcharge us."

I was going to complain but seeing the expression on Sturges' face made me change my mind. Luke and I watched him canter forward the hundred yards to the river. The marshal touched the brim of his hat as he passed a granger in a wagon heading in the opposite direction towards me and Luke. There was a woman sitting with him in the buckboard and I thought of Ma and Pa and Mister Coates. I felt the sadness and pain of the past day return and remembered the urgency that drew me thus far to this moment.

I saw the marshal get the ferryman's attention when he touched the badge on his lapel and opened his long coat to unveil his fancy twin pistol rig. The two started chatting, but they were far enough away to be out of earshot.

Luke said "How-do" to the granger and the woman as they drew near, so my interest abandoned Marshal Sturges. The man pulled back on his reins and slowed his team to a halt. He and the woman looked young enough to have been my parents years ago when they first ventured west to start a life and family of their own.

Robert skirted nervously round beside me to keep Janey between him and the wagon. His donkey ears perked high. I wasn't sure what to say, so Luke coaxed his horse closer. "You folks come across the ferry?"

The granger didn't respond right quick. He eyed Luke and his badge first and then fumbled to remove his hat in a rush when he realized I weren't a man. "Sorry ma'am. I... I didn't know." Luke gestured towards the ferry again, prompting the fellow to answer his question. "We crossed only now. Although I think that coxswain charges a little much, being that his boat is a might less than sound. A good day to you both."

Luke tipped his hat, introducing himself as Deputy Barrientos. "This is my friend, Miss Mae Kepler."

I reached out to shake the granger's hand, but he wouldn't take it. The woman with him gave me a courteous smile.

"Headed to town?" asked Luke.

"You seem mighty young to be a lawman asking questions, Mister Barrientos."

"Old enough to ride and shoot. A man must start somehow, don't he?"

The granger put his arm around the woman. "That is so. We're doing the same. Staked out some property nine miles north. Going to the land office to make it official."

"A cause for celebration," I said, eyeing the woman again, guessing her age wasn't all that far removed from my own.

"Congratulations," added Luke. "Weld is two, maybe three hours from here in a wagon. There's a lady named Johnson in town who'll probably put you up for the night if you're married. Separate rooms if not." The woman pulled her mitten off to proudly reveal a thin wedding band.

Luke proved his value as a detective when he asked the pair if they'd seen any cattlemen headed north.

"Drovers off the trail east, pushing a thin herd. They were headed north," the granger confirmed. Luke's and my eyes connected, and I realized we were on a righteous path. The couple rode on, so we trotted forward to meet Sturges, having given him plenty of time to fix a price. Got there as the marshal folded a two-dollar bill and slipped it into his breast pocket.

"Shouldn't you be paying him?" I said, re-thinking my decision to remain out of earshot of that particular conversation.

"Never you mind, Miss Kepler."

"Nothing to mind if you settled on a fair price," I said.

The ferryman told us to dismount and led us and our animals onto the timbers that formed the shabby, flat hull of his ferry. I could feel my boot-heels squish into rotten wood as I got Janey and Robert situated. "You ever do maintenance on this craft?" I asked. The ferryman glanced at Sturges before he replied.

"All it needs do is float, missy." He un-looped the line from the post that held us to shore and began tugging his passengers across.

"You want to tell him, or should I?" Luke said, removing my thoughts from the seaworthiness of our boat and back to our purpose again. I shared with the marshal what the granger and his wife had reported. Told him it was Luke's idea to inquire.

"That's good work, both of you. But don't get your hopes high. Plenty of cowboys working herds between here and the Nebraska line. All of them riding north to the railroad like us."

"Might have been them," I said, resting my hands on Janey and Robert to keep them calm.

"Could be, Miss Kepler. The trail will show. It only reveals the truth."

Once our feet were on solid ground again, we led the animals to a watering trough just below the mercantile with the fancy name. I wanted to see that Café and ask the folks within if they too might have seen our fugitives.

"You mind?" I said to Luke with a gesture towards the establishment.

"Marshal and I will take care of these beasts," he said, with a glance at Sturges.

After a pause, the marshal nodded as well. "Of course, Miss Kepler. Go on," he said.

I wasted no more time, me stepping around a sturdy gray stallion who was also tied beside the same trough. I climbed a set of wet timbers cut into the muddy slope like stairs to the little shop above. When I got close to the door of the place, I realized it didn't have no glass windows. Only burlap covering the openings to keep some of the chill and the flies out.

Inside it was dim and smelled like a combination of cat piss and sorghum. Weren't but one room with a counter and syrup barrels for tables. Three legged stools sufficed for chairs. A pot belly stove glowed with warmth from a small coal fire, but nothing in the place seemed finished.

Or very fancy.

The cat was fat and asleep on the counter where a man stood

writing with a pencil in a broad-paper ledger.

"May I help you?" he asked, not looking much in my direction.

"I wanted to see what a café looked like," I said, and he turned as I spoke.

"Thought you was a petite man in that hat and coat when I noticed you enter. But you ain't no man, are you?" He picked up a bottle and poured a little something in a small glass. "You thirsty?"

"No sir but thank you sir. Like I said, curious is all. Is it always this busy in here, Mister?"

He guffawed. "You're polite and funny too, ain't you? I got plenty of customers. My place may not be much, but all are welcomed."

"Well, I guess I am one at least," I said.

"It's only official if you part with a little coin, ma'am. Besides, I got the Indian. He's a regular. And them fellers you're riding with… maybe they'll come in too for a look-see and a sip of my whiskey?"

The barkeep's words spooked me. Making me realize there was another patron in the place I hadn't yet seen. Man was sitting at one of them barrels, his face and form hidden in the shadows. I nodded to acknowledge him, not knowing if he gestured in kind because of the lack of light. The mysterious customer's silence caused me to speak again.

"Do you have something other than whiskey?" I asked, concentrating again on the man by the counter.

"Nothing other than water and coffee, ma'am. Could make you a fresh pot if you can wait. Got dried fish hanging in back."

"May I ask another question, sir?"

"You the law or something?"

I shook my head, wondering if maybe I should leave. "My friends… them two outside. They are the law."

"Really?" He walked to the nearest window and pulled aside the burlap enough to peek. "What is your question?"

"You seen any suspicious men recently? Maybe cattle-hands looking like they are up to no good. Three of them. One of them was a big feller with a ginger beard. Goes by the name Little

John."

"I seen a girl in a man's coat and hat with a big old pistol bulging in her pocket."

I blushed, feeling all sweaty and stupid like a kid again.

He chuckled. "I'm poking fun, little lady. Giving some back." The keep wiped the palms of his hands against the front of his shirt like he'd done this many times. Looked out the window again. "Saw a group of men and a boy... two... no... three days back might be the ones you're looking for. Big man, like you describe. Boy didn't say much, but the other two they came in with were a curious sort."

"How do you mean?"

The barkeep turned to look at me. "For starters, those fellas had similar names. One went by Frank; the other was called Francis. He was a squeaky little man. I'd be careful. They both seemed a brick shy of a full load."

He pulled the burlap from the window a little farther, taking in the details of my traveling companions. "That young fella out there with the ears. I never seen him. But the one with the friendly smile and the black hat; he was with them. They shared a half bottle of my whiskey and were jawing. Sometimes whispering. Sounded like they was parleying about cattle and jobs and such."

I moved beside him so I could see Luke and the marshal the way he was seeing them.

"You sure?" I said, thinking again about Harry Sturges and his private little conversation with the Ferryman.

"Without no doubt, ma'am. That one by the big dapple; he definitely ain't no officer of the peace."

CHAPTER 8

I PAID THE barkeep for a half portion of whiskey and drank it down fast, feeling its warmth slide down my gullet. Groping to feel for that dead boy's pistol in my coat pocket, I thanked the man and walked back down to where Sturges and Luke were waiting beside our mounts. The sturdy gray was still there, so I supposed the stallion might belong to that Indian.

"You buy a cup of fancy tea in the café?" Luke asked.

"Nothing fancy about that place. Go look if you want." I eyed Harry Sturges to see how he might react, looking at him for something I missed. Something that would indicate he was someone other than who he said he was. But he kept grooming the hairs of his dapple's mane.

I started filling my two canteens worrying what I should say or do about the new facts related to my current situation. Wondered what the truth was and what wasn't.

"Time to move on," announced the man I was no longer certain was a marshal. "The trail will get cold if we dawdle. And I believe we need to get three or four more hours of riding in before we set camp." Sturges placed a boot in his stirrup and swung his other leg across his big horse's rump. "Well, come on you two, let's go. If this expedition takes too long, I intend to increase my fee."

"You done that before our negotiations even started," I said, as I tightened the caps on the canteens and looped them across the back of Janey's rig.

Luke laughed at my supposition and lit up onto his saddle too. "Maybe I should've asked Miss Mae for more? What do you think, Marshal, sir?"

"Business is a personal thing. You'll never get more than you ask for – unless, of course, you take it." He squeezed the heels of his boots against the dapple's flanks and got that horse moving north quick.

"Come on Mae. Unload the iron, we'd better go," said Luke, riding off to follow Sturges as I re-checked the harness around Robert's neck. Didn't take me long to catch them both on Janey. She was old but was a pretty sure-footed mule.

The first part of the afternoon ride was quiet. I guessed Luke was temporarily all talked out. He rode beside me, Janey, and Robert without babbling on much. Sturges led this time, now roughly following the path of the river northeast towards Nebraska at a brisker pace than earlier. The country was much the same. Miles and miles of rolling prairie with a narrow trail laid out across it. We saw another family of settlers heading in the opposite direction. An older couple and two little ones peeking out of the cover of their prairie schooner.

But they had nothing new to tell us.

Shortly after, my stomach began to growl something fierce. I pulled out Ma's biscuits, thinking of her as she often was… hands and apron full of flour. I said a prayer for her – and one for Mister Coates too. Not knowing if Doc Lowry had been able to help them.

I passed some biscuits for Sturges and Luke to have. Sturges offered up some of his jerky and Luke gave us each an apple in return. We rode on, washing it all down with swigs of water from one of my canteens. I kept my eyes on Sturges, still wondering if that barkeep had been right about him. Perhaps he'd somehow mistaken him for some other smiling, shady character?

We went another few miles and Luke spotted a rider to the west. A man on a big gray loping parallel to us. Luke said he was armed with a rifle slung across his back. I couldn't see the weapon, but I saw the man wasn't wearing no hat.

Sturges slowed when he realized we were watching somebody. "That's not one of your killers, is it Miss Kepler?"

"Mine all had wide-brimmed hats and long coats."

He pulled out a leather canister with one of them spyglasses in it. Extended the device and held it to his eye. After a moment he told us it looked like an Indian feller.

"Might be the man I saw back there at the café. Barkeep said he was one – although I couldn't vow it to be true. Too many shadows inside for me to get an honest look at him."

"Probably Cheyenne," said Luke. "Lots of them wander these parts."

"Where do you get all of this information?"

He flashed an expression of annoyance at me. "People."

I frowned.

"Okay... okay, from the sheriff... if it makes you happy. He and I have spent many an hour talking of such things. Sheriff Conley's traveled all over the territory. Says those Cheyenne that are still around mostly don't want trouble. Not like before."

We rode and watched that Indian, and he rode and watched us until he chose to move off and disappear beyond our line of sight. We kept on along the trail for another hour until the sun set, and the brightest stars started poking out through the evening sky.

CHAPTER 9

STURGES SURPRISED ME when he gave Luke his rifle and sent him out to find something for supper while he and I picketed Janey, Robert and the two horses. When we were finished securing the animals for the night, I asked why he'd given Luke his long gun. "I heard you tell him in no uncertain terms to *never give your weapon to no one you don't really know.*"

He broke a smile and took me in with his eyes again. "Luke isn't the one I worry about."

"As if I'm so dangerous," I said, feeling uncomfortable, folding my arms to hold Pa's coat closer against my frame.

"You are a woman, and women are always dangerous."

I realized he and I were most definitely alone standing out there in the twilight. I moved to get away from his gaze and slow down the beat of my heart. Found my kit where I'd left it on the ground and began pulling out my new skillet and kettle.

Without anything more being said, Sturges went looking for wood to burn while I cleared a spot to build a small cookfire. I got out some of the taters and onions I'd brought and emptied one of my canteens into the kettle.

After a time, Sturges returned and stacked the wood he'd gathered. I helped him get a fire going, keeping the pit between

43

him and me. "What if them killers are near?" I asked. "Won't they see the flames?"

He looked out at the prairie and up at the stars. "We'll keep it small for cooking and put it out before it gets too dark. You brought plenty of blankets? It'll get mighty cold out here each night."

We stopped talking when a rifle report interrupted our conversation. The mark of the same sound that took my pa's life and nearly killed Mister Coates as well.

A shiver went up my spine.

"Don't worry, that's Luke with the Winchester," Sturges said. "It's a carbine. That shorter barrel gives it a special sound. Hope he found us something good for supper."

Little John's short Spencer had been a carbine as well.

I nodded, needing to see Luke again. Not wanting to be alone with Harry Sturges no more. We listened to the silence a moment together sitting, separated by the little fire until the normal sounds of the prairie night returned.

"You asked about blankets. Got me two and a slicker. And I suppose I can sleep in my daddy's coat."

"If you brought extra stockings, put them on. I promise you it will be cold. Probably frost in the morning."

We dragged our saddles closer to the flames. Luke's too. And arranged our bedrolls in a circle by the time the boy returned with a lanky jackrabbit. Sturges told him to skin and dress it. I cut up the taters and onions and dropped them into the water before setting the skillet onto some of the hot embers. Luke added the bits of meat and bone, and Harry Sturges surprised us both when he added a pinch of flour to thicken the broth and pulled out a pepper grinder and a small sack of salt.

"Fancy for a lawman," I said.

"More than you know, Miss Kepler. I do have a taste for the finer things in life when I come across them."

He still had his pistol rig on, but the pepper grinder was in his hands. Luke had started cleaning the bore of the Winchester. I was tired of hearing about what I now believed were Harry Sturges' versions of the truth. I didn't trust him no more.

And needed to know what was real.

So, I reached in my pa's coat pocket and pulled out the old revolver, cocked the hammer back and leveled it at Harry Sturges' handsome smile.

Luke's eyes grew wide. The skillet simmered, and light from the little campfire flickered with oranges and yellows across our three faces as we sat in a tight circle.

The pistol felt heavy in my hand. Sturges stared at the tip of its barrel then his gaze raised just enough to look me in the eye. "1848 Colt Dragoon. That's a hell of a thing, Miss Kepler," he whispered.

"Mae, what... what are you doing?" said Luke.

"You're no federal marshal and I'm guessing your name ain't Harry Sturges neither."

"Says who?" he replied with little expression or emotion.

"Says the owner of that Dry Goods and Café."

Sturges' gaze narrowed, still staring over the length of my pistol, straight at me.

"He saw you three days ago sipping his whiskey and visiting with them three fellers and the boy who killed my pa and shot my ma." I stood slowly, keeping the revolver pointed at his face. He didn't say nothing and didn't move. But his eyes revealed how hard he was thinking on a plan to somehow get out of an intolerable situation.

Luke started to mumble some words of warning at me.

"Shut your trap, Deputy, or I'll shoot you too," I said to the boy sternly as I could without taking my aim off Harry Sturges.

Luke didn't speak no more.

I told Sturges to stand and remove his pistol rig. He hesitated, like maybe he wanted to explain things. I lowered the gun, aiming it at his loins and Sturges abided, doing what I proposed – setting down the grinder, unbuckling his rig and slowly sliding the strap out of its broad clasp. But before I could react, he flicked the length of that belt at my hand.

It stung when it struck. I was afraid to lose hold of the Colt and drop it.

So, I pulled the trigger.

It went off with a terrible bang and a flash and a lot of smoke. But the charge was damp, and the ball gained no velocity. It rolled out the end of the barrel and plopped into the skillet of rabbit stew with a pathetic splash. Harry Sturges let go of his belt and guns and swatted the pistol out of my hand. Stepped across the fire. Grabbed me by the collar.

I felt a sharp pain at my waist and realized he'd stabbed me with a short blade. Warm liquid began to pool against the top of my trousers, and inside my blouse and coat as Sturges lowered me to my knees. He kissed me, hard and wet on the mouth, before letting me slump over onto my side where I must have passed out.

When I woke Sturges was standing over Luke striking him in the face with the butt of his Winchester. I knew that boy was going to die and that I would too. My pa's death would have no resolution and my ma, if she were still even alive, would never know what became of me after I ventured out onto the prairie to find her husband's killers.

Sturges cussed at Luke, calling him a *Mexican smarty-pants,* and struck again. Luke began to gag on his own blood. I groped in the dirt to find a rock or a stick. Something to fight back with. But what my fingers found was the grip of the 1848 Colt. I lifted it and pulled the hammer back, whispering a prayer for Pa, Ma, and Mister Coates too.

"Harry Sturges… whatever your name is," I gasped. "You get away from that boy."

He laughed when he saw the gun. "Go ahead Mae Kepler, shoot me with that rusty piece of shit." He lifted his rifle again to strike Luke a final blow. So, I pulled the trigger a second time. There was another flash and a bang, but this time the revolver worked as it should and knocked me back in the dirt. My ears rang something terrible and when I rose, Luke was still laying at the far side of the campfire gulping and gasping for air through his swollen lips and broken nose. Sturges had fallen beside him, lying there with the crown of his skull blown off.

The pistol slipped from my hand and flopped to the dirt. I rolled onto my back feeling cold, my hands holding my wound. I looked up at the night sky and the brilliance of all the stars that had come out.

It was a peculiar thing, when I also saw the face of a gray horse and the form of the man who rode him - both gazing back down at me through those same stars above.

CHAPTER 10

I OPENED MY eyes to the sound of a donkey angry and hawing. A tall Indian man wearing a curious sombrero, lurched with disgust as he tugged on a rope tied around the ass's neck. I reckoned it was Robert. His long ears pointed straight forward like daggers and his eyes were circles of wrath. My Robert wanted no part of that man. I felt I should rise and help, but when I tried there was a terrible pain and a pulling in my side.

My body felt stiff. Sweaty too, but in a good way because I was warm beneath a layer of pelts. Beaver and coyote all sewn together like one of Ma's soft quilts. I was in some sort of lean-to framed with rough cedar posts and covered with prairie sod. It had a firepit near its center burning what looked and smelled like buffalo chips.

The man seemed to be wanting to get Robert out of the weather. Because the shelter was partly open on one side, I could see heavy snow falling and the fresh layer that had blanketed the ground beyond. I didn't see Janey or the horses.

"Do you know where my friend is?" I asked after forcing myself up on one elbow. My voice croaked like a leaky church pipe organ. The man relaxed the rope he'd been heaving and gave Robert some space so the brute couldn't bite him.

"The woman must remain still, or the wound you possess may decide your fate," he warned.

48

I touched the bandage wrapped around my waist and had a flash of memory. Recalling Harry Sturges' face close to mine and smelling the breath on his lips. Feeling the force of his hands grabbing me, and the pain of the blade he thrust in me. Him kissing me.

The shame and disgust I still knew.

"I buried the one who tried to kill you. The devil you shot. The boy with the badge is with the horses and your mule in my stable. Those animals will keep him warmer against the chill of winter." He studied Robert a moment before facing me again. "The burro wouldn't fit. I wanted him inside so the freeze would not end his journey before its natural conclusion."

With a look of disgust, he let go of Robert's rope and came close to me, squatting beside the mound of pelts I was under. His body moved with grace in silence, like when a barn cat stalks a mouse. The man removed his odd, flat-brimmed sombrero, allowing me to finally see him. He wasn't yet old, but the lines etched in his face were deep and his skin was darkened by the sun and weather.

"Did you find any dollars on the dead man?" I said. Me knowing I didn't have many left. And realizing all the money I had started this foolish enterprise with was the sum of what my pa had struggled to save.

"If there was anything of value in his pockets... this has gone with him to the world of the dead below — for I do not have it."

A shiver passed up my spine, me praying what money I still had might stretch far enough to finish the task I'd pledged to complete.

The man squatting beside me shifted with an obvious uncertainty of his own. The two of us inches apart and yet still no more than strangers to one another. His hair reminded me of the color of coal. I noticed it fell to his shoulders and not below — nowhere near long enough for a braid.

"Are you a real Indian? You don't look like one."

He laughed a gentle laugh, revealing his teeth, bright through his smile. I saw sadness in his eyes that made me think of Pa. The fear that I might never see my ma again in this world returned as well. "I don't mean nothing by it, sir. But I think I saw you at the café. The keep there… well, he said you were one of them. We glimpsed you again watching us from a ridge. Luke thought you might be a Cheyenne."

"Luke's the boy with the badge?"

"He is. Will he be alright?"

"Your friend was badly beaten. He'll sleep for many hours. Don't know for how long or if he'll live. But rest, and the warmth of the other animals will be his best medicines. Not unlike yours."

"How long have I been asleep?"

"Two nights have passed since I found you by the campfire."

"I apologize for asking, but do you have any food? I'm feeling a terrible hunger coming on."

He shook his head. "You may drink but must not eat… not yet. Your insides must begin to heal."

"Will I die?"

"When it is your time, you will die. All of us will. Know that your wound is serious but not deep and that I have prayed for you." He moved to the fire and poured something out of a kettle into a small porcelain cup which he held in both hands as I sipped from it. I must have made a face when I tasted the steaming liquid.

"Tea from roots. The brew will quench your thirst and push you back into quiet dreams." Robert shuffled forward out of the snow on his own accord. The man smiled. "Your burro does what he wants and knows what he needs."

"He's a fine ass," I said, remembering the first exchange I'd had with Harry Sturges. Even then he was pretending to be something he wasn't. Standing there behind Mrs. Johnson's boarding house in the dim early-morning light with messed up hair and a stupid handsome smile on his face. I felt Sturges kiss me on my lips hard again. I heard the pistol shot, felt the gun in my hand, and saw Luke, in my mind, lying by the campfire struggling to breathe, Harry Sturges dead next to him with the top of his head blown clear.

I done that.

I closed my eyes. Shut them hard for a time. The Indian stayed beside me in silence watching. Don't know how much time passed before he spoke again.

"You asked me who I am. My Christian name is Thomas."

I opened my eyes and, as he continued to speak, his hands moved with elegant gestures that matched the rhythm of his words. "I am not from that distant territory the white man calls India. And my people are not Indians. We are Tonkawa and have shared much of this land and the places in it for many generations." He swept his arm in a great arc encompassing the walls of the shelter and the snowy prairie out beyond the smoldering fire.

"Tonkawa?" There was something special about the word as I repeated it. It felt proper and suited him well. "And you are a Christian?"

"My mother is. She is old now. My sisters are Christian as well or at least they were when last we spoke. I have two of them and have not seen them in many seasons." Thomas took my hand in his, squeezing it gently. Robert shuffled his feet. His ears drooped and he crept closer, sniffing at the two of us together.

"What is *your* name?" Thomas whispered.

My eyelids grew heavy, but I held myself back from the edge of what I knew would be a deep valley of slumber. "Mae," I whispered. "Mae Kepler."

"Good to make your acquaintance, Miss Mae Kepler. In truth, I am a man with two names... and some say, two spirits. In Tonkawa, my people call me *Walks-Like-a-Feather*."

CHAPTER 11

WHEN I WOKE again, my donkey was gone, and Luke was lying beside me. There was a bandage about his head and across one eye. The boy wheezed with each breath as his chest rose and fell beneath a cover of animal pelts like mine. I propped up on one elbow again. Walks-Like-a-Feather slept on a pallet opposite, on the other side of the firepit. A dim glow of embers remained. The prairie outside was silent, covered in a blanket all white and illuminated by a three-quarter moon.

I figured it must have been four days gone since Sturges stabbed me and beat on Luke. My hunger was powerful, and it didn't take me long to notice a covered pot of broth simmering at the edge of the embers. When I lifted myself up, my hand clattered against an empty bowl and a wooden spoon. My wound pulled, feeling plenty sore. But I was drawn to the thought of that broth like a bee to a flower patch and it smelled good when I poured some into the bowl.

"Slowly, Mae Kepler."

The Tonkawa rose from his pallet to squat beside me.

"You certain your name ain't Sleeps-Like-a-Feather?" I mumbled, between slurps.

I could see his teeth again through a grin. "Your stomach will grow angry if you eat too much. And yes, I do not often slumber like a bear. When you live alone this is best."

I asked about Robert, and he told me my burro was sharing the stable with Janey and the horses, now that he'd brought Luke in with us. "The boy has rested long. Perhaps being closer to us will rouse him. He must wake and have nourishment soon as well."

It was cold and I was so tired. I began to shiver after taking in some of the broth. Walks-Like-a-Feather put me back beneath the covers and pulled them tight around my body. Don't know how many times in the night I repeated this – sipping the broth and then sleeping. By daybreak, the urge to relieve myself became as powerful as the hunger in my belly. All that broth wanted to come out.

Walks-Like-a-Feather helped me slip on my boots and led me out in the early morning sunshine. My boots crunched in the unbroken snow nearly thirty steps to a spot beside a small grove of saplings. I squatted, letting go, balancing myself against the branches. When I was done, he took my hand and we returned to the relative warmth of his shelter. I didn't want to sleep anymore, so asked if there was something I could do.

"Speak to your friend. Like you, he must wake, or may never will."

I sat close to Luke so we could keep each other warm. Walks-Like-a-Feather covered my shoulders with some of the pelts and I took the boy's hand in mine. "What should I say? He's the one normally does all the talking."

"Tell him what you see, what you feel, hear and smell. Let your senses lead your words. Perhaps your voice will pull him back from the place where he dreams."

"Not sure I am so familiar to him."

"He risked his life to join in the pursuit of whatever it is you seek."

I studied Luke's face as he slept beside me. I could see him better now that the sun was bright and glittered off the snow outside. His lips and nose weren't as swollen but had grown all blotchy with ugly shades of purples, yellows, and greens. Walks-Like-a-Feather left me alone with him for a time, telling me he needed to find fodder for the animals, or they might soon die as well.

I watched the Tonkawa leave and figured I'd better start speaking to Luke. "That man has got two names," I told him, not really knowing where to begin. "He seems to be a kind feller. Don't make me feel unsafe, neither... like some might. You know how they do, busting from their sockets to spy a woman's bosom, midriff, and bum." I squeezed his hand a couple of times. Felt the heat rising off his forehead with the back of my own. "I believe he's like you. Raised proper and respectable. Although it is a little odd, he lives out here all by himself."

Walks-Like-a-Feather had made coffee in my new kettle. He had an old set of woven mittens setting besides, so I used them to keep from burning my fingers and poured myself some. I guessed he'd found the grounds and wares in all our provisions we stowed in the saddle packs.

I let Luke have a sniff as he lay there breathing. It steamed and was strong and tasted bitter but went down easy. "It snowed last night," I said sitting close to him again. "About eight inches. You need to wake up so you can appreciate the shine on all that white-washed beauty out there. The sky too. It's a deep blue and the prairie looks so very clean. Like my ma's going-to-church spring blouse."

Luke suddenly smiled and his lips started moving without no words escaping.

"You awake? Figuring to tell me something?"

He coughed out a laugh. Small and sweet. His voice was hoarse like mine had been. "I said... I bet your ma is as pretty as you. Especially pretty in a white blouse."

"Oh, shut your mouth," I whispered, feeling myself grow flushed. He grinned and I gave him a gentle shove of annoyance. "I liked you better when you were asleep."

Luke didn't open his one uncovered eye, but it didn't matter. The boy had spoken and was coming 'round. I propped him up with some of the pelts from my bed. Coaxed him to sip a little broth, which he did. Got him to take five spoonfuls before he nodded off again with a smile on his hurt, cracked lips.

"Thomas!" I shouted. "Luke spoke and I got him to eat. What should I do?"

Walks-Like-a-Feather came running, leading Sturges' big

dapple and told me to stoke the fire. He brought the other horses, my mule and donkey out as well and picketed them in the snowy meadow near the open side of the shelter. We boiled water and gave Luke a bath with a cloth and dried him with one of the fresh blankets I had in my bedroll – the one I'd kept on Janey. I scrubbed his soiled clothes in a bucket until I became too tired, and blood began to seep again from the wound in my side. Walks-Like-a-Feather finished my work and stretched the damp articles across the lowest bare branches of saplings to let them dry while the sun was still strong.

"I will get some yarrow for your wound, Mae Kepler. And wash your clothing too. You smell as bad as the boy."

My nose confirmed my pits were ripe and I knew he was right. I gave a scowl anyway and drew my knees up to my chest where I sat beside Luke and the fire. "Not sure that's proper. For me to be naked in the presence of a man who ain't kin. What shall I sleep in? Got only one outfit."

"I have a long shirt. Wear that until your things dry."

"I'm sure being a single man out here all alone - that'd be convenient."

Now he scowled. "Mae Kepler, I see beauty in you, I truly do. But not in the way a husband desires his wife, or a man longs to be with a woman. Yours is like a smooth rock that glistens in a bubbling stream." He paused and shuffled his feet.

"Your courting is lackluster, if you're trying to sweet talk me out of my britches." I looked him in the eye, confused by what he'd said. Walks-Like-a-Feather took off his hat and stared at the ground, turned the brim round and round in his hands.

"You are safe with a man like me."

My eyes dropped to the ground. "Some folks say I'm not very pretty," I said remembering Little John's words again.

"That's not true. I think you are."

"Then why am I so safe?" I asked gazing upon him again. Wanting to witness some sign I did not yet see. "You don't like women?"

"I do. Why wouldn't I? I... I just don't wish to lie with one."

"So, you prefer a man for company? My pa told me of such things. Said a feller was hanged for it down in Fort Worth."

55

Walks-Like-a-Feather was silent a moment before he spoke again. "What if I do?" He spoke to his feet instead of me and kept rotating the brim of that funny hat.

"My ma and pa taught me the dictates of the Bible. Luke 6:37 says *It is not for us to judge.* That's a promise from Jesus in the New Testament. He never said nothing about a man loving another man good or bad… other than *love thy neighbor.*"

"I know His words, Mae." He lowered himself down beside me. Drew up his own knees, mirroring my pose, and rested his hat on them with a sigh. "The Lord offers powerful medicine and knows no bounds," Walks-Like-a-Feather said and closed his eyes. "It's other parts of the Bible that set wrath in the hearts of those that run me off. Why I dwell out here alone."

"Is that why you have the two names?"

"Two lives woven like a braid. Some of each part are only memories and others persist - always with me in the here and now." He gestured out at the landscape again. "The prairie helps me come to terms with who I am. Its challenges keep me sharp and alert. Its beauty reminds me to love the Tonkawa I was created to be."

His words were a comfort. Gave me pause to study him a moment more before I spoke again. "All I need know is you're a good example of a man," I said. "You saved me and this boy. That's the proof for me and Jesus. Course, I'd still prefer you stand yonder while I remove my garments." I nodded towards the big dapple and the other animals.

Walks-Like-a-Feather looked worn and tired from the four days of nursing he'd been doing. He placed his hat back on his head and did as I reckoned, paying attention to the livestock while I removed my soiled things and covered my dignity with his long shirt. He added snow and lye soap to the boiled water and let me wash in private. When he returned, he stirred my clothing in the same pot; rinsed and hung them from the cedar rafters above us.

By then, the sun had set, and the sky grew dim. Walks-Like-a-Feather returned the animals to the stable and retrieved Luke's garments, now stiff and dry. I helped him dress the boy before he gave him more broth and bundled Luke for the night. I felt the chill of the prairie air and Walks-Like-a-Feather bundled me as well. He withdrew to his own bed opposite mine with a groan. The steady crackle and glow from the embers of his small fire lulled us all into a deep slumber.

CHAPTER 12

I DREAMED OF Harry Sturges. Him, Little John and that boy in the blanket. Them two fools named Frank and Francis weren't in it. Sturges put his arm around my shoulders and smiled before I felt his knife cut into my side. He pushed me towards the big man with the beard, who struck me across my chin with his Spencer rifle. The boy laughed while the two men dragged my ma away. "Meet us at Jacob's Ferry when you're spent," Sturges shouted before he was gone.

The boy seemed scared until he grabbed me by the collar and began ripping and popping the buttons off Pa's coat. I realized I wasn't wearing nothing beneath and knew he intended to have me. His lips parted, and he leaned to kiss mine, until blood began gushing out his mouth. Didn't seem like Mister Coates was there with me, but his hand appeared, spiking a blade through the side of the boy's throat like he done before. Then my dream slid away to darkness.

"Find them, Miss Mae," a voice said to me clear and distinct.

I swear it was Sturges.

I awoke in a sweat, wearing nothing but that long shirt beneath them pelts, feeling awkward when I remembered I was sleeping in a place with two men I barely knew. The dream reminded me I'd lost four days and the snow that had fallen had covered the only trail I knew could lead me to those murdering scoundrels. I looked at young Luke sleeping and knew it was my fault that I'd gotten him mixed up in such difficulties. Walks-Like-a-Feather too – poor, exhausted man. My presence in his home, well I figured my welcome had grown thin.

I pushed the warm pelts back and stood shivering in the darkness, thinking of Ma. Seeing her in my dream made me realize I might never be granted a chance to ever be with her again in this life. All that violence now four days or more gone. Time I'd squandered by letting Harry Sturges get his hands on me and Luke.

Little John and his rabble were my problem. I needed to stop mending and wasting time and get on out there again. Finish this thing one way or another.

Though my wound still ached, I did not care. I quick-retrieved my smoky clothes from the rafters, passing repeated glances at Luke and Walks-Like-a-Feather to make certain them two weren't gazing at my womanhood when I peeled off the shirt. I checked the bandage still wrapped about my waist and redressed with every garment I had. Even took the worn pair of mittens Walks-Like-a-Feather kept beside the kettle to keep my hands from freezing since, like a fool, I had none of my own.

In silence I grabbed the Winchester Sturges had carried. And a box of his cartridges too. Then crept out toting the carbine and my saddle bags to head for the stable across the cold ground to retrieve Janey and Robert.

Out on the prairie there were bald patches where some of the snow had disappeared. These had frozen again, turning the spots hard like granite. A glow from the moon filtered through a cover of clouds to shine a little light. Enough for me and Janey to guess the way forward.

It felt good to be on the move again. And to be alone, with only myself to fret about. Course old Janey wasn't a happy mule out in that weather. And Robert less so. The donkey tugged on the rope tied to my saddle to make sure I knew how dissatisfied he truly was. But each of them tried to step with care – that's what mules and donkeys do. It was all unfamiliar ground where holes might be hidden beneath the places still covered with snow. I had the Winchester slung across my shoulders and the box of cartridges stuffed down in one of Pa's deep coat pockets.

We must have covered a mile or more and were going nearly at a trot by the time Janey stumbled and I heard her leg snap as she fell. I was thrown over her head and shoulders and caught the ground hard. I felt my wound split at my waist. Janey bellowed a horrible scream. Robert hawed, afraid for her and uncomfortable out there in the open, and in the cold darkness.

Janey snorted, trying to catch her breath. She wanted to stand but her broken front leg folded forward on itself, and she screamed again in pain. The bone ruptured through her hide at the knee and blood began to spurt out onto the dimly lit frosty ground. I looked upon Janey with horror, seeing her eyes wide with fear.

I believe my Robert began to cry. I'd never heard the sounds he was making coming from any animal before. He began tugging at the rope and hawing loudly and furiously. In a panic I stood, cut the rope thinking it might calm him down, but the donkey ran off out into the dark until I couldn't see him no more. Only hear his cries as he circled about in the distance.

I dropped to my knees, tears in my eyes. Shed them mittens from my hands with my teeth and slipped the Winchester off my shoulders. Janey screamed again trying to rise, not understanding why she couldn't and why she was in such agony. There was nothing I could do to calm her, and I knew she might hurt me if I tried to hold her down.

I'd never loaded the rifle in my quiet haste to not wake Luke and Walks-Like-a-Feather. I felt for the tip of its muzzle making sure it hadn't been plugged with sod when I hit the ground. Tried wiping the tears from my eyes, then fumbled with the box of cartridges only to spill them across the frozen ground beside me.

Robert was still out there, hawing and crying. Loping in a broad circle, unseen on the dark prairie. I plucked a single cartridge from the icy ground. My hands shaking, the tips of my fingers now numb.

I wiped my eyes clear again and shoved the round into the loading gate of the Winchester. I stood feeling wobbly, as though the ground was shifting. Cocked the lever and aimed the bore at Janey's head knowing how much of my life had been spent living with this faithful mule. She and Cobb had been the only team that had taken Pa, and Ma or Mister Coates, and me into Weld on so very many occasions. This end... her end was my fault. I forced myself to focus just on Janey and her suffering, looking down the rifle's barrel. Breathed out, held the air in my chest like my daddy had shown me.

And squeezed the trigger.

I'd never fired a Winchester before but was too close to miss. Course the kick knocked me down worse than the 1848 Colt. I rose again, looking at Janey's form with the rifle in my hands. Robert was hawing less. Maybe calming down since the mule had gone silent.

My hands were raw, so I began groping for the mittens I'd flung. When I only found one, I stuffed my other hand into a pocket and moved to Janey to make sure she had truly passed. With a single purpose, I unbuckled the saddle bags and tugged them off, draping them around my neck like a yoke. Using one arm to press against my torn gut, and the other cradling the long rifle, I began walking and calling, knowing if I didn't get back to Walks-Like-a-Feather and Luke, I'd soon be dead too.

"Robert! ...Come on!"

The prospect of returning in the darkness without him wasn't favorable. He hawed a response, sounding farther away than I figured. When I found Janey and Robert's prints etched in the ground, I felt a little relief for I knew these would lead me back. I picked up my pace calling the donkey's name again - hoping he'd follow.

I lost sight of Janey's remains in short order. The steps I took warmed me a bit, and soon Robert appeared, having sense enough to abide my voice and join me. But it weren't because he was lonely.

Robert leaned against my shoulder, nuzzling. He felt warm to the touch. "Your fine. Nothing to worry about," I whispered.

The donkey's ears were low making me think something else was wrong. Something I didn't understand. I took hold of the piece of rope that trailed him, so he couldn't run again, and slung the saddle bags across his hips. He blew air through his nostrils and kept looking back out across the dark prairie from which he'd come.

That's when I spied a wolf. He was big and sat down where he stood when I spotted him, like he was telling me not to worry. But Ma and Pa had told me stories about wolves from when they'd traveled west. Said don't be fooled by no lone wolf.

Ain't no such thing.

I spun to look about and in the opposite direction found four more sitting like the first. They weren't as big but were watching and waiting just the same, at the dim edge of my perceptions. I lifted the Winchester to aim at them and broke into a sudden sweat despite the chill. I'd left all the cartridges back by Janey, where I'd spilled them in the snow.

"Shit."

I tugged at Robert, getting him to turn. "Come on," I told him with a stern voice. We made haste to follow our own prints back towards Janey.

The wolves stood as one, matching our pace, parallel about twenty-five yards out. The big one to the right and the other four to the left. It didn't take me long to realize they weren't precisely walking parallel. They were getting a little bit closer every four or five steps. Taking their time, angling in. Being all relaxed about it.

When they got to fifteen yards, the whole group of them disappeared, running ahead, growling and yipping with excitement. I needed those rifle cartridges, so me and Robert kept walking in the same direction, now following the wolves. By the time I saw Janey's form through the dark, it was too late. The pack had started in on her and there were more of them now. Ten or twelve. I expect the ones in charge were eating first - tearing at Janey's flesh, while the young wolves laid back, taking to watch me and my donkey again.

I knew then, there weren't no way I was going to get the shells before them wolves got me. Course Robert was more than pleased when I tugged at him to back off and turn tail. But them young ones followed, seeing opportunity and the chance to sample their own supper. I had a knife and nothing else of use with me except Robert and his rope, an empty rifle, and no pistol. I held the blade in one hand and re-slung the Winchester, coaxing the donkey behind me.

Seven wolves came for us. Growled and circled 'round. Inching closer, tightening their noose, and baring their teeth.

CHAPTER 13

I FLUNG MY knife away, realizing it weren't a proper tool for fighting so many wolves. With the Winchester pulled from my shoulder and ready, I clubbed the first one who tried to bite Robert. Hit him right across the snout. Made the beast yelp and whine. That set them all back a moment, until they came again, bolder, and even more determined.

There was a shout in a language I didn't understand - a familiar voice in the night. The wolves and I turned to see Walks-Like-a-Feather arrive on his stallion. The Tonkawa fired a shot at the night sky that flashed across the prairie from his saddle. When that didn't do nothing, he reloaded and dropped the nearest one with a bullet through the chest. Me and Robert retreated to him in disbelief, watching the pack scatter into the black.

"Not sure if Mae Kepler is stupid or head-strong," Walks-Like-a-Feather said. I let the Winchester fall and began to sob. Plunked to the frozen ground still gripping the rope looped around my donkey's neck.

"Don't call me stupid," I said, knowing he might be right. I'd killed Janey in my haste to finish quick what I'd taken on. Same as I'd done to Harry Sturges. Walks-Like-a-Feather dismounted and came to me. Got me on my feet again and brushed off my backside.

"I bet your mother is strong-natured," he whispered. "Your father too. I believe I see what Deputy Luke has discovered in you."

I picked up the rifle from where I dropped it. "My pa was murdered six days ago. Ma violated and left to die. That man I shot... the one you buried. He knew the three that done the deeds. I fear if I wait to mend any longer, I'll lose the trail that will lead me to them killers."

Walks-Like-a-Feather put his arms around me. Held me tight a moment before relaxing his embrace. "Mae Kepler, those men are still out there. You'll locate them in the flesh or beneath a shallow grave. I have no doubt of this."

Then he took Robert's rope from me, leading us to his gray.

"How... how did you know to find us?" I asked, watching him tie the burro to his horse.

"You and Luke wore me down into a deep slumber this night, but a rifle report travels a good distance out here."

He helped me climb up, him mounting behind me on the gray. The stallion knew what to do, whirling himself around so we could follow our own tracks back across the icy plain to shelter and safety. And there, we slept for hours under warm covers until the sun was halfway across a blue sky.

I opened my eyes smelling fritters popping and sizzling in a skillet. Walks-Like-a-Feather was doing the cooking and had made a fresh pot of coffee. He'd already set aside a stack of the golden corncakes on a porcelain plate. That hot food made me crawl out of my cocoon.

"Where did you get such fancy dishes?" I asked, sliding to join him at the fire and was surprised to see Luke hunched there too, beside him. "You're up?"

"I am. The plates are from his mama," the boy explained. "I already asked."

He looked better, except for them big ears. Sitting and munching on a fritter, holding up a tea saucer so I could see its

65

delicate, painted design. Walks-Like-a-Feather gave me a sideways glance and nodded at the kettle.

"Mae Kepler. Looks like you need coffee."

I responded by fumbling through my pockets to find the one mitten I still had and used it to keep from burning my fingers. Luke handed me a cup, which I filled, topping off theirs as well.

"Your face ain't so messed up," I told Luke.

"You look good too."

I took a sip of the brew and swallowed to shade the fact that I'd appreciated his compliment. "Didn't say *you* looked good... just that you weren't so messed up."

Luke passed me the plate of fritters with no respectable rebuttal.

Walks-Like-a-Feather rescued him. "Mae Kepler may not offer many gifts of kindness but is honest with her words." He touched the back of my bare hand. "You lost one of my mittens, didn't you?"

I pulled away, feeling ashamed. Remembering again what I done. My ride across the prairie through the dark night, Janey's fearful cries, and the snarling of the wolves.

"I... I... not exactly." I looked at his hands and mine. Couldn't tell if he was angry or annoyed or a little of both maybe when he replied, keeping his gaze on me.

"So, you have the other one?"

I shook my head. "I know where it is," I said with a gesture towards the prairie. "...Near Janey."

"Since you don't want to waste time healing, perhaps you can work for your bed and board this day. Take Luke after you wash and put away the meal. Ride and recover my mitten and when you return, I will show you how to treat that fancy rifle you now possess with more respect." Walks-Like-a-Feather stood and moved to a corner of the shelter, not waiting for me to respond. He began gathering several baskets as if sorting them and deciding which one of the woven objects to use. "If I am to join in tracking these killers," he continued without looking in my direction. "...you and the boy must learn to fight with a little more observation and a lot less daring."

"I'm not a boy and I can shoot," argued Luke, who was

already slipping on his boots.

"I'm sure you can, Deputy. But shooting is not the same as fighting."

"Wait. Are you saying you'll join us?" I asked, hearing only what Walks-Like-a-Feather had said about maybe helping us.

He looked at Luke before replying. "I have not yet decided to knot my fate to yours, Mae Kepler. But if you are both willing to work hard... practice new skills and recover for a few more days... perhaps."

I gave him a hug before we left to find his mitten, feeling a renewed sense of hope. His embrace made me think of Pa again and the locket he'd shown me the day he was gunned down. The one Little John had stolen.

"We'll ride quick," I promised.

"Quick is not necessarily good. Ride with care, mind your injuries, and don't waste all your time conversing. A little silence might attract something better than your mother's moldy biscuits for our supper."

Luke prepared his bay, and I readied the dapple, although Sturges' tall gelding wasn't too sure about me at first. My donkey wasn't happy neither, watching me place a saddle on a mount other than Janey. Robert started sniveling, his contempt making the dapple even more nervous. I paused to scratch him behind his ears, knowing he didn't want nothing else familiar lost anytime soon. Luke knew what to do, giving Robert two turnips to raise his spirits, and provide enough distraction for us to slip out onto the prairie without him for a time.

The snow was all but gone, so the trail that led to Janey was thin. Mud returned to the prairie with the warmth of the sun, making the horses slip and slide some. Neither of us was entirely sure we were going the right way until turkey buzzards appeared, spiraling high above. Luke spotted their formation, and the birds revealed the way to the place where Janey had passed. When we got close, we saw more buzzards on the ground pecking at her remains. Others were flapping about the dead wolf Walks-Like-a-Feather had shot. Them big birds were squawking and pecking at each other over mighty sparse pickings.

I dismounted, shooing the buzzards, and searching the

ground until I found the missing mitten and even the knife I'd discarded.

Luke tucked his peacemaker pistol in his belt and dismounted too. "Maybe I need to name you *butter-fingers?*" he quipped as soon as he spied the box of cartridges I'd spilled. "Dropping things all over the place… it's amazing you managed to hold onto that rifle."

I tugged at the dapple and led him to where I could help pick up the scattered ammunition. "You try loading a Winchester when it's cold and dark and your ride is screaming at you because she's broken her leg and you know you're the one responsible."

Luke came near, his eyes meeting mine. He didn't give me no hard time about losing Janey like I figured he would. Luke poured the cartridges he'd gathered into my coat pocket and patted them tight against my hip, his hand lingering there a moment. When he leaned close, I noticed how his presence felt good to me in a funny way.

Not like Harry Sturges.

Luke smelled clean like soap and savory like bacon grease.

"Mae… I… I'm sorry for the circumstances. But I am glad we met," he whispered.

I'm sure I blushed. I didn't know what to say. "Well, I'm glad Sturges didn't kill you," was all I could muster - even though I was glad we met too.

He took my hands in his and looked me in the eye. "I don't know what happened back at that campfire so many nights ago. I don't remember much. But I am happy to be alive. I'm still out here living and breathing in a place where I get to spend more time with you."

I admit my heart fluttered, but I stumbled again for the words to reply.

When he turned to go back to his horse, Luke stopped halfway there and turned to gaze back at me. "You're going to load that repeater now, right?"

I swallowed hard, still feeling awkward and warm, and nodded. I shoved a dozen of the cartridges we'd collected into the loading gate until the Winchester's magazine was full.

"That's the way," he said after I was done. "If we get caught in a fight, you reload that thing every chance you get. And keep count of the numbers so you don't ever go empty again."

"Says the boy who's been in so many gunfights."

Course I regretted the poke as soon as them words sprang forth from my mouth. Me seeing the bruised expression on Luke's face.

"Mae Kepler, I already told you I hadn't ever shot at a man, and that was the truth. I am no pistolero. I've arrested a lot of drunks and disorderlies. Cowpokes and ranch hands and such. But I did get shot at once. Fellow tied one on like all the others. Except this time, he pulled a derringer, shot, and missed. My forty-four was loaded, and I had every right to put that man down. But I didn't want to kill *him*. Not a fella going through something bad. Someone suffering a situation I had no cause to understand. I decided to punch him in the throat instead. He turned blue from lack of breath, and I dragged him to the jail where Sheriff Conley dealt with him later."

"Luke... I... I'm sorry for making light of such a thing as shooting and killing. You done right for that feller."

I watched the boy as he rode his bay, leading us back to Walks-Like-a-Feather's place. Me thinking about him taking my hands in his. His kindness. Me acting sharp and stupid. I worried again about my ma and Mister Coates. And what I was supposed to be truly doing way out in the middle of nowhere amidst the Colorado prairie.

Luke and I watered and fed the livestock when we returned. We said nothing more to each other and rested by the fire until Walks-Like-a-Feather appeared riding his gray. Carrying two sage grouse. Them birds were alive, tied together at their feet and he showed us how he'd used woven traps to catch them instead of wasting ammunition and calling attention to his whereabouts.

He had us kill, then pluck and dress the birds. Showed us where to hang them to cure. Then Walks-Like-a-Feather took us down a culvert into a dry creek bed where we practiced some with the guns. First, we took them apart – spread the bits out on a blanket. He watched us like a hawk while we took turns disassembling the Winchester, Luke's .44, and my 1848 pistol several times. The old Army Dragoon looked and felt a whole lot better when we were finished stripping and cleaning it.

Luke showed me and Walks-Like-a-Feather how to take out and repack the cap and ball, although I still only had the makings for four shots. We had a little more than 100 cartridges for the Winchester, so each of us practiced using twenty rounds. Shooting at rocks and twigs and prickly pear. Walks-Like-a-Feather fired ten himself since he was already good with his own breach-loader. I told him he could have the fancier repeater when we were done - if we caught Little John and his cohorts. He wouldn't confirm one way or another if he'd made up his mind to come along. But I do believe the prospect of that carbine pleased him.

When the sky grew dim, we returned to prepare supper, which we did together. Walks-Like-a-Feather roasted the grouse on an iron spit. In the skillet I cooked the rest of my taters, onions and a few wild oyster mushrooms we'd discovered in the culvert. I put Luke in charge of peeling and cleanup. Course Walks-Like-a-Feather eyed him to make sure he didn't crack none of his porcelain.

Next day, Walks-Like-a-Feather brought us to a place out on the prairie that was broad and flat. The soil was firm – good for practicing the riding tricks he wanted us to try. He told Luke and me to dismount and watch. And after, with no explanation, he rode off at a gallop, and returned riding hard, straight back at us, disappearing from sight then reappearing moments later.

Luke and I laughed nervously. I think we even clapped. "My pa taught me how to ride and rope some. Ain't no way I can do that fancy bit," I shouted as the dust settled. "I'll land on my tail and bust everything."

Walks-Like-a-Feather smiled. I don't think he favored my apprehension, but he didn't argue. Luke stared with great curiosity. Like he was witness to the most mysterious of carnival acts.

"Watch again," was all that Walks-Like-a-Feather said before he turned his gray to ride a distance away a second time. At thirty paces with his horse at a gallop, he spun and kicked, getting the stallion to return full-on again. With yards to spare, the rider disappeared while his horse kept charging. Came so close clumps of earth and mud showered over Luke and me. The horse thundered past with an empty saddle, as if some magical power had been called upon to make the man vanish.

Course when Walks-Like-a-Feather turned back, he held his position to reveal the skill of the feat and what he'd done to do it – crouching low, one foot in the stirrup and one hand clutching the side of his cantle – plainsman hideaway style. He pulled himself back up in the saddle and pointed his gray at us so we might parley. "Years ago, a girl who was a friend taught me that. She was an Arapaho. Her people were some of the best riders I have ever seen."

Walks-Like-a-Feather could tell I was still not ready to give it a whirl. He urged his horse closer to where I could feel the warm breath blowing hard through the stallion's nostrils.

"Like I said, if I give that a go, you'll get nothing but me busting my bum. Probably start to bleeding again."

"Maybe this one isn't a trick for a girl, anyway?" interrupted Luke. He lighted onto his own horse, "But I am definitely going to give it a try."

"Shush before you do, mister tall-in-the-saddle," I barked all annoyed and turned to Walks-Like-a-Feather. "Exactly how old was this Arapaho girl? The one that taught the trick."

He dismounted when I asked but became distracted by something there in the dirt beside us. He removed his sombrero, filling it with small stones he selected off the ground. Then placed them in a simple circle around a lone wildflower that had somehow labored late to push up through the harsh ground.

Walks-Like-a-Feather smiled when he was done and stood, returning his hat upon his head.

I felt my impatience return. All I wanted was to ride north again to find Little John and his rabble and must have worn that frustration on my face.

"Mae Kepler... our lives are journeys. Much more than the sum of the tasks each of us completes." Walks-Like-a-Feather looked out across the plain like he knew what I was thinking. He turned, uniting his gaze again with mine: "To answer your question, the girl was eleven and I was ten."

"A child? Younger than me. What became of her?"

"We parted ways after our communities joined for a time. I learned many things from her. She was good at teaching," he said while he checked his horse's flanks and legs and hooves, then caressed the gray's face above his nose. "We met once more after the girl had grown to become a woman. Some years since, word came from down Texas-way that she'd been killed by the white man's soldiers. Her people and mine are scattered now – taken by the Army to the reservations, or west to shelter in the mountains. That society is lost, but its lessons... like the ones I share with you..."

Walks-Like-a-Feather shifted, leading his horse beside Luke's and stepping close enough to me to place a hand on my shoulder. Sharing the weight of his words. "These are powerful medicines, Mae Kepler, that can benefit us in ways we may never realize. Or be ones we call upon sooner than any of us might suppose."

He removed his hand from my shoulder and touched the flank of Luke's bay. Smiled at the boy before turning back to me. "Especially when the three of us ride north together to seek justice or death for the men out there who killed your father."

CHAPTER 14

TWO DAYS LATER, crisp and dry and early, Luke and I followed Walks-Like-a-Feather on horseback, north across the prairie. We loped with a purpose towards the State of Nebraska and our sole destination — the cattle town of Ogallala — as the rise of the sun cast streams of oranges and pinks before us. The clear sky and our lightly packed kits afforded us faster travel and the best chance to catch the scoundrels we sought.

I looked back to check on Robert when we passed the spot where I'd lost Janey. His donkey ears drooped low in recognition of the place, though only scattered bones of my mule and the wolf remained. I don't know if it was the location or a smell in the breeze that made him think on it. Robert was happy enough when we didn't delay and moved on. His ears perked and flit about like normal once the trail and terrain became fresh and unfamiliar again.

I watched Walks-Like-a-Feather handle his gray. The horse was smaller than the one I now rode, Sturges' tall dapple, but was more sure-footed. Almost wild in its nature, Walks-Like-a-Feather's stallion took each rise and subsequent downward slope along the trail with confidence.

We rode for seven or eight miles with Luke at our rear, and me pulling Robert riding center spot. The sun rose and warmed the prairie more than it had done since the snow had fallen and melted days before. After some time, Walks-Like-a-Feather led us down through a shallow hollow, where a crick ran, and a cabin and a small stable had been built on the rise beside it. There was a wooden gate and a split fence enclosing a cozy yard. Walks-Like-a-Feather raised his hand to halt us. Instinct and a sense of dread told me to dismount when I realized the front door to the house had been left open.

By the time I slid the Winchester from its scabbard, Luke and the Tonkawa had dismounted as well. All my thoughts focused on that open door, which made me recall my own home, its front entrance left ajar only a week before, when so much violence had changed the course of my life.

"The gates of the stable are open too," Luke whispered, strapping his pistol belt about his waist. The gates had been broken apart, one twisted off a hinge.

"Hold the animals, Mae Kepler," Walks-Like-a-Feather said softly. "Keep your rifle trained on that front door."

With his own long gun in his grasp, and after a gesture for Luke to go opposite, he skirted right. The boy drew his .44 and scurried low along the fence line left. I bound all the bridle leads to a post. The three horses and Robert watched me with curious eyes as I aimed the Winchester at that doorway. Recollections of my dead dog lying in my own yard, the echo of two rifle shots, and the painful moans of my ma's suffering, made my throat go dry.

Walks-Like-a-Feather peeked in the stable first while Luke covered him from the side of the house. He did the same in return for Luke as the boy lighted onto the small porch and slipped inside the cabin using silence and care. I heard Luke call, his voice threaded with despair. Walks-Like-a-Feather ran to him, while I untied the horses and Robert and followed, leading the animals across the homestead's yard.

Them two didn't want me to go inside, but I shouldered the carbine and pushed between them anyhow, needing to know.

Wanting to see.

A mother and her daughter had been left on the tidy dirt floor within. Both dead and preserved by the cold. Naked and violated.

74

Butchered in a place that, only days before, had been their humble home. I turned away. Fell against Luke who holstered his pistol and took me in his arms to hold me there a moment. I wanted to pretend I hadn't seen it, but the sight of the two women was etched in my mind.

"We need to check for anyone else," whispered Walks-Like-a-Feather. I released myself from Luke's grasp, knowing he was right, and forced myself back to kneel beside the women while they searched the property. I couldn't help but see myself and my own mother in the shapes of their still forms. And felt first embarrassed and then angry by the way they'd been discarded. I remembered what Mister Coates had done for my own Ma and stood. Searched the place until I found blankets to cover the two. And when it was done, I knelt beside them again.

When Walks-Like-a-Feather and Luke returned, they told me the perpetrators had gone, all the livestock taken. Their tracks, several days old, leading north.

"And we found two others," whispered Luke, who knelt beside me. "A man and a boy face-down in the stream and shot, Mae. The bastards bound their hands at their backs before they murdered them."

Walks-Like-a-Feather squatted to be with us. After sharing some silence together, the three of us recited something short and simple for this family – the Lord's Prayer – a Gospel we all knew without thinking.

"It was the same men," I said, finally standing again.

"I believe you're right about that," Luke added. "Sheriff Conley says thieves and cutthroats will almost always do again what has worked for them before."

Sadness and guilt filled my soul. Tears streamed down my cheeks. "If I'd only gotten out of the wagon. Ran to hide. Or used that shotgun. I could've stopped all this then and there."

Luke took my hand in his. "You'd be dead too, Mae. Little John would've cut you down before you had a chance to use a scatter gun on him. And you know there's no place to run or hide in the heart of a cattle pasture."

"The Deputy is right," agreed Walks-Like-a-Feather, who stepped to the still-open door and gestured at all that was framed beyond it. "The paths men choose, like Luke says, *are* often predictable. But the world is also full of motion that is hard to stop. Like a stone rolling down a hillside. What happened to this family you did not cause, Miss Mae. Those men – the outlaw Little John and his rabble – they chose to get this stone rolling all by themselves. And probably first pushed it down the slope long ago."

"But if I'd done *something*..."

"All I know is you're still alive to catch them, Mae," said Luke. "And God or maybe fate led me and Thomas to stand here with you now to help with the task."

The boy gave me a soft smile. Squeezed my hand and then left us to find a shovel and dig four graves in the yard while Walks-Like-a-Feather and I wrapped the bodies with care. Soon after, I watched Walks-Like-a-Feather finish the final knot on the last of the family none of us knew anything about. I realized I'd been spending so much time fretting about avenging my circumstances, catching murderers and such, I still didn't know much about *him* - the one who saved me and Luke and kept us from being added to the register of the dead.

"Thomas," I said, speaking his Christian name. "You told me you have a ma and two sisters, but I don't really know anything about them. Where are they now?"

He tied the blanket tight, tucking the end of the wrap between the dead husband's feet. "Gone years ago, to a village along the front range," he replied, nodding west toward the Rockies. "Many of us wanted to get away from soldiers and the white man's promises of peace and plenty."

"And why aren't you still with them?"

"I told you I am a man with two spirits. One in the past that belongs to my family and my people. The other is in the here and now. Who I am and who my mother and sisters became – our notions forced us to walk apart. Down separate trails. I love them still but I'm not sure they view me in kind. Not sure they even consider me to be their kin."

"You really believe that?" I asked as we lifted the bodies and arranged them together out on the cabin's small porch like a cord of wood before burying them in the holes Luke had dug.

"I do," he said.

"Do you think you'll ever see them again?"

Walks-Like-a-Feather stood, and I followed him as we walked to the crick to wash our hands in the cold running water. "Perhaps one day. If not in this life, maybe after."

CHAPTER 15

THE STALLION'S EYES swept the prairie grass that flowed with the breeze in ripples across the plain. I watched the gray and Walks-Like-a-Feather again as they eyed the horizon and all the dangers I knew it might hold beyond its curve.

"What's out there, Thomas? What are you watching for?"

He turned to look at me, his expression serious. "The killers we pursue."

"I know that much," I said, keeping the dapple close beside his horse.

Luke rode near as well. "She's not asking about that," he said to Walks-Like-a-Feather. "We see you always watching, Thomas. Your horse does it too. What is it you are looking for out across all that ground?"

"A big question from a wide-eyed young man." He turned to look at me. "And woman."

"So... what do you see?" I asked again, pulling at Robert's lead to get the donkey to keep up, wanting to hear what Walks-Like-a-Feather might say.

"Why don't you tell me? The land around us is always

speaking."

"The prairie?" Luke rode closer still, looking doubtful.

Walks-Like-a-Feather gestured with the broad movement of his arm across the land. "All of it. Look closer at the grass on the plain... See how its blades kneel before the will of the wind. Like my ancestors before, the plains have many stories to tell and secrets to reveal."

Luke slowed the gait of his bay, keeping us all riding side by side. I thought of Harry Sturges, who'd said much the same. *The trail always reveals the truth.*

Walks-Like-a-Feather reined in his horse to pause. He gestured again at the land in front of us. "A herd of mule deer have traveled yonder, to follow the sun. The grass bends there in a different manner where the animals have walked."

"I see it," said Luke.

"You do not," I said, doubting the boy's words.

"Look again, Miss Mae. Let your senses do the work. Don't only see what is in front of you. Hear the wind as it crosses the grass. Feel the motion in the land as it rises and falls like the breath inside you."

"But the land, it ain't moving, Thomas. We are," I said, nudging the dapple with the inside of my boot to get him going again.

Luke and I followed as Walks-Like-a-Feather led us down a dip, across a gravel bed in a gully where a trickle of water ran, and a small grove of saplings rose. He nodded again at the next slope we were approaching. "The land does move, but ever so slow. Hills and valleys – even the ones far in the distance - tell old stories. Wind and water shift the soil to reveal patterns of past seasons. Scars like this one we now cross... these, in clefts where the land folds like this, they often share the news of recent storms and new life. And, if you know where to look, and what language to listen to, the plants and animals may speak of those who have passed before us by the hour, or recent days gone by."

Walks-Like-a-Feather guided his horse so close to me that his leg touched mine. He led my eyes with one hand to a spot halfway between us and the rise ahead where the deer tracks finally revealed themselves to me traveling east to west. The grass bent and moved with a stiffness distinct from all the rest.

"You're right. I do see it. I see it now too."

I looked at Luke, my excitement showing on my face. He grinned a reply.

Walks-Like-a-Feather nudged his horse forward to keep us going and we kept after him, sticking to him like pine sap to ask more questions.

"How did you know the deer caused them tracks from so far away?" I asked.

His eyes met mine: "Your ma and pa taught you how to leave your mark... how to sign your name?"

"They did."

He looked at Luke, who nodded the same.

"Animals do this as well. Each with a unique signature like yours, Mae Kepler. Like Deputy Luke's. And mine." He gestured at the game trail as our horses loped across. "Now you'll recognize the mule deer's mark when you spot it again." Up close, we saw the scores of deer prints, pressed by the herd as they had passed over the sod. "Bison cut deeper, dark scars like freshly tilled soil. The antelope herd leaves a path that is broad and shows less purpose, while wolves travel a narrow one that discloses order, but hides their number."

We rode for several hours more talking about what was all around, big, and small, until Walks-Like-a-Feather finally led us across the main cattle trail going north to Nebraska. We kept a little west of this road so we could watch for drovers and observe the kinds of herds they were pushing.

When the sun was high, we stopped to let the animals graze. Walks-Like-a-Feather chose a silty shelf mounded beside another small stream that was little more than runoff from melted snow. We shared jerky, apples, and a few corn dodgers I'd made the prior day. Luke and I searched for flat stones and tried skipping them across the crick while the Tonkawa sat on a folded blanket to watch. I thought of the family we'd buried in the four holes Luke had prepared for them. Then prayed my own Pa had a good spot by our own crick where Mister Coates had promised to let him lie.

And I said a prayer for my ma. In my mind I saw her still

rolling biscuits, sweeping her kitchen floor early each morning. Bringing me a small amount of hope to hold on to.

Past noon, after a short rest, Walks-Like-a-Feather told Luke to stay with the animals. "Bring your rifle, Miss Mae, and follow."

I saw disappointment in the boy's eyes for not being included. "Perhaps you should take Luke instead? I don't mind staying with the horses."

"The Deputy is comfortable with his peacemaker. Mae Kepler must be comfortable with her weapon as well, if we are to succeed in bringing justice to our enemies." Walks-Like-a-Feather took his breach-loader and strode off low, fast, and quiet, up the bank of the crick and through a small cluster of dormant prairie willows.

I looked at Luke again. He patted the pistol stuffed at his belt and motioned for me to go. I felt for the extra cartridges I'd kept in my pocket, like he'd suggested, and slid the repeater from its buckskin scabbard. "Okay, Mister Barrientos, I'll be back soon," I said, and ran to catch up, not knowing where Walks-Like-a-Feather was leading me or how long it might take.

"You are one to take a lot of side trips when pursuing fugitives, aren't you?" I said when I finally caught up. Walks-Like-a-Feather scowled and motioned for silence. He kept moving forward, allowing me to watch the way he placed his feet and where he chose to step. When I saw the motion of his body and how his moccasins made no sound with each footfall, I thought again of a barn-cat stalking a mouse and recalled the first time I witnessed him approach me beneath the shelter of his lean-to.

Below the peak of a gentle knoll, he showed me the prints of several animals who'd followed our same path. We went farther to the top where he sank to the ground, hugging the curve of the slope. Walks-Like-a-Feather bade me to lie beside him, and we spied four antelope resting in the glade below on pillows of matted grass. He placed his thumbs and fingers against his brow like a set of antlers, then touched my rifle. I took the Winchester against my shoulder, checked its load, found the buck, and aimed, holding, then slowly releasing my breath.

When I squeezed the trigger and fired, the buck stood and

leaped three times before dropping. Them others scattered at the sound, disappearing into a stretch of taller grass. Walks-Like-a-Feather led me to the one I'd killed. We knelt beside the antelope, and he had me place my hands on the animal to feel its warmth while he spoke soft words over its still form.

"A prayer?" I whispered when he was done.

"We give thanks for the life this animal has sacrificed and for the nourishment it shares."

He passed me his rifle and lifted the buck, letting it fall across his broad shoulders. I led us back, carrying the two long guns, following the same game trail through the grass.

"Your name? Your Tonkawa name... Can you tell me how you got it?"

He chuckled when I asked and walked behind me in silence for a dozen steps before speaking, as if extracting a distant memory from his past. "When I was young, before my father died, he would take me with him to find the buffalo. Much like we searched for the antelope this day, except our trips would sometimes take many hours, or days to complete. Often without success."

"Soldiers and profiteers slaughter the great herds, but when I was a boy, the bison were plentiful. Father had much time to observe me while we hunted and to teach many things. It was he who gave me my true name when he discovered I stepped with a very light foot. *Like a feather falling on still water*, I remember him describing to my mother."

"I think it is a good name."

"Yours as well, Mae Kepler. It suits you. Strong and proud and handsome."

Luke collected the horses when we returned, happy I'd gotten us the meat for supper. I went after my Robert, who'd wandered downstream. The burro made me scramble and chase him a hundred steps before stopping. He allowed me to get almost close enough to grab the rope he dragged, then pranced for another dozen yards, hawing with glee.

Two more times I did this until finally he knew I was licked. I sat in the reeds by the crick to catch my breath and he joined me, letting his rope dangle for me to take. Of course, Robert flitted his tail and bobbed his head – wanting to be delightful and all. He demonstrated a few more gentle brays as if it were an admission that would suffice. Forgiving his rebellious nature, I gave him a good scratching behind his ears to cajole him back to where Luke and Walks-Like-a-Feather waited. We secured the buck across the donkey's packs and set off again.

Despite the danger of our task and the death we'd left behind, I enjoyed much of that day, riding with Luke and getting to know Walks-Like-a-Feather. Learning about the signs all about us that had always been there but that I'd been too ignorant to see. The prairie rolled on for a time. We spoke less as we grew tired, and by late afternoon the plains were broken by a spine of rock, and farther, by a string of more distinct hills. Walks-Like-a-Feather slowed his pace again and Luke and I fell in beside him.

"Tell me what you see," the Tonkawa asked.

"The ground is changing," I said.

"It's late in the day," quipped Luke. "Are you saying we should be looking for a place to camp for the night?"

"I have not said anything. I asked you to *tell me what you see*."

I pulled my reins in and stopped the dapple in his tracks. Robert breathed out heavily through his nose, displeased he'd carried the extra weight of a dead buck all afternoon. But then I noticed his snout rise to sample the smell of the breeze. His ears perked. Luke pulled left and circled back to join me. Walks-Like-a-Feather kept his horse traveling forward and quietly spoke a set of instructions over his shoulder.

"Keep on. Follow my pace but look to the leeward rise."

We did as he asked, catching up and setting our horses to a similar gait. Luke and I saw men on horseback, silhouetted against the sinking sun.

"Those aren't drovers, are they?" Luke said.

"Not cattlemen, nor are they Miss Mae's fugitives. They are Cheyenne. Three real ones, Deputy Luke. Probably hunting. Keep moving with a purpose and the warriors may not bother us."

The Cheyenne watched from the ridge like Walks-Like-a-Feather had done the first time we'd spotted him. I was curious about them but recalled what Luke had said as well about their disposition: "They *mostly* don't want trouble... not like before."

But these men chose not to stay clear. Within minutes the three launched down the slope, pushing their painted mustangs to catch us on the thin path we'd been following towards the Nebraska border.

Walks-Like-a-Feather unsheathed his rifle and pointed it at the first, speaking sharply with words I didn't understand. Luke's horse instinctively backed away, placing more ground between it and the three unfamiliar riders. My donkey moved close to the dapple, who stood firm. The big horse had no intention of yielding ground to the smaller rides of the newcomers.

While Walks-Like-a-Feather continued to exchange strong words with the first Cheyenne, one of his companions rode to me, circling around with a keen gaze. Robert snorted his displeasure when the hunter touched the dead buck roped across his packs. The Cheyenne took me in from the crease of my hat to the tips of my boots like I was an animal up for auction at the county grange.

He shouldered his rifle and patted my horse's rump, saying something about the tall gelding to his friends. He drew close, right alongside, eyeing my face and pawing at the material of Pa's coat.

"Careful, Mae," Luke warned.

The warrior grabbed my lapels, lifting me out of my saddle with a tug. Before I knew what his intentions were, he yanked the sides of my coat open - I guess to see what might be hidden underneath. Luke shouted and tried pulling his forty-four. But the third Cheyenne would have none of that, and raised his own rifle, pointing it at the boy.

Now, it's not like I were naked under Pa's big coat. I wore my shirt and undergarments beneath. But like my ma, I been blessed with a reasonable bosom. Easy enough to bury beneath an old, loose overcoat. But the fact of my true nature became quite obvious to them Cheyenne when they eyed my curves through the fabric of only a blouse and chemise.

In the blink of an eye, anger rose within me. I saw my ma again, exposed and left for dead beneath our kitchen table. And them two - the woman and her daughter - curled in cold silence and discarded like rubbish on the floor of their own cabin.

I hauled the 1848 Colt Dragoon out of my pocket and shoved it in that Cheyenne feller's face before he had a notion to conduct any more such unsolicited investigations beneath my garments.

"Might want to rethink your strategy, Mister," I said.

When I cocked the pistol's hammer back, I figured my intentions didn't need no translation.

He withdrew his hands, coaxing his horse away from mine, retreating some seven or eight feet. Walks-Like-a-Feather threw more words, and them two other Cheyenne all of a sudden started to laughing. I straightened up and gathered the halves of my coat together keeping the pistol trained on the one beside me, who, by then had decided the moment was amusing too. Everyone was smiling, but no person seemed ready to lower their weapon.

Walks-Like-a-Feather broke the impasse by nudging his horse closer to mine. "Maybe it's time you tried that horse trick, Mae Kepler?" he whispered. The Cheyenne kept pointing their rifles, us still pointing our guns back at them too. "Do it slow and with deliberate intention. Show them you're not a woman to be touched or trifled with."

I gently lowered the hammer on the Dragoon and eased it back in Pa's pocket. The Cheyenne all looked at one another with a little surprise. I passed Robert's lead to Walks-Like-a-Feather so he could hold the donkey. Then I kicked Sturges' horse to running.

Luke called to me with fear in his voice, I suppose afraid the hunters might shoot. But the big dapple leaped, and the sounds of his trampling buried any message. Four strides later the gelding was galloping full bore.

I held the reins tight in my fists, leaned low, feeling the horse's mane whip against my face. I pulled hard, swung the dapple around, gaiting him back toward Walks-Like-a-Feather, Luke, and the three Cheyenne. In a cloud of dust that was my own making, I disappeared right before their eyes.

My fingers burned as I held on to the cantle and horn of my saddle to hide my form behind the horse's. My foot floated in the single stirrup and my body bounded up and down, in harmony with the rhythm of its hooves. I felt the healing wound in my side pull tight when I yanked the reins again to turn about so the men and boy alike could see I'd done the hideaway trick proper and true.

"Eye yee, yee, yee, yai!" one of the hunters shouted. The others pointed their weapons high and fired shots at the setting sun while I hauled myself back in the saddle. Everyone rode to meet me with excited voices, making me feel suddenly special as I received a litany of praises thrown at me in three languages. Luke arrived first beside me, wrapping me in his arms across our two saddles. Walks-Like-a-Feather and the Cheyenne circled 'round.

"The woman is warrior," exclaimed the lead hunter. He nodded at me. "We honor you as brother does sister."

Walks-Like-a-Feather shouldered his breach-loader and swung off his horse, reeling my donkey and the dead buck close. Luke figured to know what he was planning and dismounted as well to help him sling the antelope to the ground. The Tonkawa quartered the carcass with his long knife, passing the biggest cuts on to each of the three hunters. Resecuring the last portion across Robert's rump for us to keep for our own supper.

There were no more words exchanged. Them Cheyenne rode with the meat we'd shared, back beyond the rise where we'd first seen them. And we set to traveling north towards the border again, to find a suitable place to lie for another night beneath a brilliant sky.

CHAPTER 16

ANOTHER DAY PASSED and the weather grew bleak. We'd ridden for several hours under a shroud of clouds by the time we heard a whistle echo across rolling hills. Luke about fell out of his saddle. "A locomotive!" he shouted with delight and a thick grin. "May I ride ahead to see it?" That boy bubbled with excitement.

I shrugged my shoulders. "You've spoke on it enough these past days."

"Ride on, Deputy," added Walks-Like-a-Feather with the flick of a hand.

Course he did not hesitate. Luke kicked his bay into a gallop, hooting and hollering. He rode to the next rise, no sooner beckoning us to come join him.

"Your man is calling."

"He ain't never going to be no such thing while he is under my employ," I told Walks-Like-a-Feather. "That boy's still between hay and grass… barely a man, anyway. With big ears and a penchant for conversation. And *he's* calling *both* of us."

"Yes, ma'am."

I looked to Robert. "Come on, you brute, we best pick up our pace and see what this commotion is all about." The donkey

87

hawed and raised his head up and down like he was a little annoyed, but he did what I asked, and we all cantered to meet Luke at the top of the slope.

The train was in the valley below. Luke mused that it was an *"invention beyond all others."* And it *was* modern and magnificent; I'd heard folks speak of such newfangled marvels, but without a doubt this iron beast was like nothing I'd witnessed before. Belching black smoke out of a tall funnel stack as it chugged up the grade. Once it cleared the top, the locomotive spewed less soot and followed the line on down to a small town that was several miles in the distance.

Luke pointed at the engine. "It's a 4-4-0," he proudly announced.

"That how much the thing weighs?"

"This machine must be many, many tons, Miss Mae," said Walks-Like-a-Feather.

"Weight has nothing to do with it," explained Luke. "Train engines are about axles. See the small wheels up front and the big one's underneath the place where the men are working?"

We both nodded.

"Four little wheels, four big ones," observed Walks-Like-a-Feather.

"Exactly," said Luke. "The big ones push the engine. Give it strength. They are called *drive wheels*."

"What about the last number?" I asked. "You said *4-4-0*."

"The newest models have wheels behind the drive wheels – I expect to support the weight of a heavier boiler. I bet this one came from Philadelphia. A company there named Baldwin makes most of this type of locomotive back east."

"Sheriff Conley tell you all this stuff too?"

"No ma'am. I read about it in the *Rocky Mountain News*."

The engine tooted again, announcing its arrival.

"You think it's the train Little John will use to move the stolen cattle?" I asked.

"Only one way to find out," said Walks-Like-a-Feather, and we all coaxed our horses down the gentle hillside. Then followed the iron tracks towards a crowded community built around not much other than a train depot, a dozen old Army tents, and a dozen more freshly milled wooden structures.

Walks-Like-a-Feather told us the place had taken its name from the Lakota Sioux. Pronounced "Ogah-LA-la," it had become one of the newest boomtowns in Nebraska and a terminus where Texas and Colorado cattlemen delivered herds to ship east and west by rail.

He pulled his sombrero down low to shadow his face and hunched in the saddle as if he were becoming a different sort of man. Then motioned for Luke and me to lead. We entered the main street south of the rail line suddenly immersed in a bustle of men and horses, wagons and cattle, all ankle deep in mud.

There were soldiers from the United States Cavalry, cattle punchers, prospectors, and more than a few drunks. So many people and so much activity along the row made my head reel like a spool on a loom. The women we witnessed on the street were mostly whores – and not like the few staying at the saloon back in Weld. These Ogallala ladies were bawdy and bold, flashing their wares in doorways and the open flaps of big, weather-stained tents. Cooing and cawing to coax anyone who passed by within.

Stores and shops all seemed to be in various stages of completion. Some with tarps for roofs, others covered by canvas and tar, or with overlapping sections of tin. Folks along the edges of the street argued vigorously over prices. Discussing quality and dates of delivery. We rode past two scruffy laborers pushing and shoving, coming to blows, while only four paces on, seven more stood in a loose circle, laughing and joking.

Farther down, we spied a whole group of folks none of us had ever seen before. Said they was from across the sea in China. Come to build the railroad and never left. They seemed to have their own shops and wares. Marked with signs and words none of us could read.

On we rode until we came to an establishment beneath another weather-worn tent called *Drover's Store*. Seemed a place appropriate enough to find answers to questions about cattle and cattlemen... maybe rustlers too. We secured the horses against a hitch rack out front, and Luke offered to water and feed them while we investigated inside. I adjusted my own hat and the cuffs

I'd rolled to shorten the sleeves of Pa's coat. Impatience began to rise within me again.

Inside, I led Walks-Like-a-Feather through a noisy crowd of smelly men, straight to a counter that was soaked in beer. More men were loitering there two or more deep. Course none of them parted enough to let us speak with the tender.

"Perhaps you should purchase a drink?" said Walks-Like-a-Feather in my ear.

"Me? You're the man."

"I am as such, but the color of my hair and skin may not be favorable."

I realized many of the men in the crowd were staring. Not at me, for I could be one of a dozen of them in my floppy slouch hat and heavy coat. But no one else was dark or as striking as Walks-Like-a-Feather. They were pale and shabby and nearly all seemed, to me, to be unshaven drunkards.

"Maybe you should go back out?" I said from the side of my mouth. "Luke can trade spots. You know he'll do it."

"I want to make sure you are safe."

The crowd was stirring. Growing deeper. So, I didn't argue and pushed to get closer. Walks-Like-a-Feather kept his hand on my shoulder and moved as I did to stay near.

"Watch yerself, boy," one patron complained. Another shoved and glared. He made a fist but let me pass when he saw the Tonkawa towering behind me.

The keep at the counter wore wire glasses and a brimless wool cap on his head. I raised a hand, "Can I get a drink?"

He looked at me. "Beer's all I got this day."

I nodded and the barkeep grabbed a metal cup from the stack beside him and proceeded to wipe it dry until he noticed Walks-Like-a-Feather, who now rested his hands on my shoulders like a guardian.

"Lookahere, young fella. You can't bring that Injun in my place. His kind ain't welcome."

The crowd of men around began to gripe. Murmuring like they was in agreement with his judgement. "But he's my friend and he ain't no Injun. Thomas is Tonkawa. His people been here long before you and your kin. Mine too."

The keep would have none of my justifications. He set the cup down and pulled a short scatter gun from beneath the long counter. "I'll blow you and your fancy Tummy-Cowin' friend plum into the street if you don't git now... I told you, no Injuns. So, git."

Man next to me echoed the same sentiment. "Yah heard the gentleman, now git."

My eyes caught the barkeep's one last time. He raised that gun and squinted. Walks-Like-a-Feather squeezed down with both hands, taking hold of my coat and shoulders below and pulled. Dragged me out of there before I could speak another word and before that gathering could turn decidedly mean against us.

Back in the street, Walks-Like-a-Feather told me to mount my horse quick. "Deputy, you untie yours and hers and let's find us something more hospitable."

No sooner had we started riding when we heard shouts and hollering behind. Some feller spouting off about killing the next Injun he spied. Someone else telling him to *hush* and to find himself another sip of something back inside.

Down the way there was another establishment named *Aufdengarten*. It sat at the intersection where the main cattle trail led south, back to the Platte and the Colorado Territory. The smaller print on the sign read, 'Dry Goods, Groceries and Liquor'.

"Maybe this place'll be better?" I asked.

A dark man sat on a pickle barrel outside wearing a tattered Union coat, a long braid, and a faded Union cap. I could see him acknowledge Walks-Like-a-Feather with his eyes. The Tonkawa touched the brim of his sombrero to acknowledge him back before he replied. "Might be our best option, if we go inside promptly."

"He one of your kind?" asked Luke, swinging off his horse and untying his holster from his saddle to place it about his waist.

Walks-Like-a-Feather shook his head. "Pawnee. His people come not far from this place."

We hitched the animals to another public rack and the man on the barrel promised to watch them if we liked. Said he'd do it for three bits. I dug in my pouch for a coin. Luke said no. "After is best. When we're done."

There was less of a crowd and the barkeep within had a different manner about him and spoke as if he were from somewhere far from Nebraska. Luke removed his hat when he spoke to the man and ordered a couple of beers - one for me and one for him, even though it weren't exactly my preference. Walks-Like-a-Feather got himself a pinch for his pipe and, after I paid, he led us to a square table at the back wall of the place where the light was particularly dim. He set his hat on the chair nearest the front door and sat opposite with his shoulders against the wall. Luke and me each sat to one side like a set of bookends.

We peered about the room to see if we spied any familiar faces or suspicious characters. But the place looked like it was merely full of drinkers and players. Not scoundrels and murderers like I guess I expected.

I sniffed at my beer and Luke picked up his to take a sip. "Sheriff Conley calls these gunfighter seats," he said after wiping a little froth off his lip with the back of his hand.

"And who exactly is the gunfighter here? You?"

"Didn't suggest that, Mae," Luke said. "Just stating a fact about the chairs."

Walks-Like-a-Feather struck a match and took a few deep draws against the tobacco in his small pipe to get it lit. "Hardly gunfighters, but you both handled yourselves well when we danced with the Cheyenne. Miss Mae, *you* should mind the truth in the Deputy's words. When you're looking for men such as the ones we seek, its best to know who is coming and going from an establishment like this."

I looked at Luke. "I do recall you and your sheriff sitting in a corner like this the first time we met back home. And you, Thomas, first time I saw you... I didn't. You were hiding in a shadow, with your back against a wall."

"Maybe you are learning, Mae Kepler," Walks-Like-a-Feather said, flashing his white teeth.

I took a swill of the beer, which I did not care for. I suppose the expression on my face revealed this same fact.

"Why didn't you say something if you don't like it?" asked Luke.

"It's fine."

I forced myself to take another sip. Maybe to prove I could do what they done just as well once again. My hands were red and raw as they held the cup of beer. Walks-Like-a-Feather noticed too. "You still need a good set of gloves."

"Ain't that the truth," added Luke. "Maybe we'll find you a pair in one of the shops this town has to offer?"

I put my hands back in my lap, out of sight. Watched the folks coming and going for a few moments before eyeing Walks-Like-a-Feather again. "Speaking of truths," I said to retreat from the notion of my sorry hands, "what was it you told them Cheyenne anyway, Thomas?"

Walks-Like-a-Feather gave me a look like he didn't know what I was asking. He shifted in his seat and took another pull off his pipe. Luke set his pint down and leaned in. "She's talking about when we all had our guns cocked and ready. The Cheyenne too. Ain't that right?"

I nodded. "You said something mighty amusing to set them all to hooting and clucking like a bunch of hens."

He puffed a ring of smoke in my direction. I could see the patch of humor sprout in his eyes. "I told them you were my wife."

Luke started to laugh.

When I didn't join him, the boy frowned. Pushed his half-empty beer away before looking at Walks-Like-a-Feather. "You two doing something I don't know about?"

Walks-Like-a-Feather didn't say nothing, only re-directed his gaze at me.

"Thomas is tall and handsome for sure, but whose hands I been holding?" I said to ease Luke's suspicions.

He took hold of his cup again, staring at the brew within. His eyes narrowed and he looked again at Walks-Like-a-Feather. "If you're so handsome, what's so funny about the notion of Mae being your wife? ...Not that I think she'd ever walk down the aisle with a man like you," he blurted out with a wagonload of awkward.

Walks-Like-a-Feather straightened his back. Took his pipe out of his mouth. "What kind of man am I exactly?"

"I... I didn't mean it with any disrespect. You're a good man. But you live alone – choosing the path of a bachelor. It's obvious."

Walks-Like-a-Feather ruffled the mop of hair on the top of Luke's head, and I was relieved no misgivings had come out of all this banter yet. I looked at Luke, picturing all the promise he might hold. He was handsome enough, and I had become fond of his company. But could I love him? Could I share a life with him?

These thoughts made me think of Ma. Made me worry about her again. I looked at Luke and wondered if she might favor him too. I felt no clear answers about my feelings. At least not in that moment. And I still had no idea about Ma - if she were yet alive for such cares to even matter.

A course I had to keep pushing.

"Thomas, I'm thinking you being an attractive bachelor ain't the thing. It's the boy. I believe Deputy Barrientos is thinking maybe I should be *his* instead."

Walks-Like-a-Feather eyed Luke when I suggested the possibility - wanting to see what he'd say. Be there no doubt, I was more than a little curious myself.

Luke fidgeted and flushed, but never faltered. "There is that, Miss Mae Kepler. Perhaps I *will* marry you one day. But I anticipate it to be a union of your terms when it arrives. You'll remain a spinster long before ever kneeling as any man's piece of property."

I suddenly felt warmer than a girl ought to about a boy, trying to keep the both of them from catching on about the fact. But I believe I did let myself smile.

"Well, now, Lucas Barrientos, I am amazed how you can talk your soul out of such deep canyons." I noticed Walks-Like-a-Feather relax against the back of his chair when I said it. He took a contented puff on his pipe. I realized there might be more stink to his story about them Cheyenne laughing than he was saying, and it weren't the smell of no tobacco. "Those hunters, did you know them already, Thomas, and just not say nothing?"

He appeared a little surprised that I would ask but shook his head. "I did not know them."

"You sure?"

He sighed. *"They* know me... and the reputation I bear."

"Reputation?" said Luke, suddenly leaning forward again. "Whoa, maybe you should be careful with this one, Mae," he joked turning his gaze to me. "Old Thomas truly is a lady's man - even according to the Cheyenne. One of those *eternal* bachelors."

I looked at Walks-Like-a-Feather and him at me. And we shared a smile.

"Something like that," was all I said.

Luke finished my beer after he was done with his. There was a clap of thunder and drops of rain pattered on the canvas over our heads. I figured we'd better find a roof to stay beneath for the night and I slid my chair back. Gave Luke some coin to check on the horses and pay the Pawnee feller watching them.

"I'll join you in a minute," I said.

He nodded and headed for the street. Walks-Like-a-Feather said he'd take a moment to finish the dregs of his pipe while I returned the cups to the counter.

I guess the coming gale had chased folk home or to the camps where they resided. Only a few patrons remained in the place as I walked from our table to the spot at the bar where the keep was working. A few men were playing cards and smoking cigars across the way. Two more were sitting closer to the street with a whore whose charms were spilling out of her tattered, frilly dress. They were drinking beers and laughing. She was not.

The sound of the wet weather on the tent grew, and I slid the cups across to the bartender, my back to the place. "Thank you for the drink and tobacco, Mister."

He smiled and set the cups in a basin behind the counter.

"Excuse me sir, but if you don't mind my asking, any chance you might know where most of the drovers camp around here?"

"You looking for work?

"Might be."

"Most are up in the hills all around. They come in for liquor and company when their drive is complete. I can tell you who to speak with if you're interested in something new."

"What if a feller's waiting to sell some cattle. Where would he go?"

"The trail bosses usually assemble to meet buyers at the grange near the edge of town. It's beyond the water tank for the train. There's a livestock chute nearby as well for loading herds."

I remembered to touch the brim of my hat in the way a man might.

The barkeep invited me to come again, like he meant it. "Be careful out there."

That's when the hair on the back of my neck began to rise. The keep's eyes broke from mine to greet a fresh customer approaching. I heard the jingle-jangle of Mexican-type spurs and looked into the mirror hung on a post behind the counter to see who the owner of them spurs might be.

It was a drover, damp from the rain. He stood tall and had a ginger beard. Wore a wide brim hat and a cattleman's long coat. Stepped right beside me, slapping two bits down on the counter.

CHAPTER 17

THE STARK MEMORY of Little John's voice roiled in my ears: *Make sure they ain't breathing when you're spent.* My mouth went dry, and a lump of fear got tangled in my throat that I could not swallow. As I waited for the tall, bearded drover standing at my shoulder to speak his mind, my hand sought the Colt Dragoon cradled in Pa's coat pocket until my fingers wrapped around its cool grip.

"Maybe you got something a little stronger than suds this day?" the feller finally asked the barkeep. That's when I knew his voice weren't right. Not right at all. Nothing like I remembered from before.

The keep nodded and poured the man a jigger of rye.

Sweat broke on my forehead when I recognized the power of the anger in my heart. I forced my hand to relax. Buried the hate again as I watched the stranger pick up his small glass. He nodded kindly to the keep and gave me a nod as well.

"Fine way to end a mighty long one punching cattle, don't you think?" the drover said with a thin smile and took a sip of his whiskey.

"You need something else, lad?" The man behind the counter asked me.

I let go of the pistol and allowed my hand to return to the bar. "No sir, sorry sir. I... I thank you again for the information and the beer." I muttered "good day" to the stranger beside me and scurried to find Walks-Like-a-Feather still waiting for me at a table.

"You almost killed the bearded one, didn't you?" he said, not looking at me. He slipped his pipe and tobacco together into a small pouch.

"But I didn't," I said. "I held until I knew it weren't him."

"What if it *had been* Little John? What then?"

My shoulders slumped because I knew his words were true. Killing a man on sight in a saloon was no part of any plan to bring justice down on those I sought.

Only vengeance.

Walks-Like-a-Feather pushed the table forward and stood, placing his hand in the small of my back. "What you did was good, Mae Kepler... using your senses to seek the truth. When we do find these killers, remember a bullet to the chest can't be your first action. Corralling and catching them, standing these men before a judge - this is the medicine that will invite peace back into your life. Maybe replace some of those dark dreams at night with brighter ones."

He and I glanced at the tall drover still leaning against the counter, chatting with the barkeep, alive to enjoy his drink. I felt relief and a sense that maybe I *could* do this thing. Control my desperation to find my pa's killers. Finish what I'd pledged to God and Ma, Mister Coates, and even Doc Lowry. And I would do it in the way I promised Walks-Like-a-Feather.

With more observation and less daring.

"We'd best see after Deputy Luke before that boy gets washed away," said the Tonkawa, and I followed him towards the door.

He and I peeked out at the rain that had drenched everything beyond. It was nearly night and hard to see through the dim weather. The muck in the street was being replaced by dark puddles, though the main drag was not entirely absent of town folk. Others were doing much the same as us — standing beneath rooflines and inside canvas covers, peering out to watch the weather blow.

"Do you see Luke?" I said as we huddled at the edge of the big tent and felt the rain turn to sleet as the icy spray began to prick against our faces.

Walks-Like-a-Feather's expression revealed his concern.

"I do not. The animals are gone as well," he said.

"You think the Pawnee took him somewhere?" I said, now worried about Luke too… and the whereabouts of my donkey and the horses.

The pickle barrel that feller had been sitting on was tumbled over. The barrel moaned like a spirit of the dead each time frozen gusts passed across its broken bottom.

Not a moment later someone poked me with a stiff finger in the square of my back. "You two misfits wondering about that boy with the tin star?"

We spun to find the girl who'd blurted them words out standing up close behind us. Petite, wearing soggy dungarees, and blinking at us with the bluest eyes I'd ever seen. She was shorter and younger than me. Soaked to the skin from the rain.

"Our town sheriff took your friend's pistol. Said he intended to ask him a few questions." The girl pulled her dripping hair back as she spoke, tightening the bandana she wore to keep it from sweeping across her face.

"You saw this?" I said.

She nodded. "We ain't got no jail here yet, but…" She pushed her way between Walks-Like-a-Feather and me and pointed out into the storm. "I'm sure he took the boy and them horses to hold them up the street in the Washburn Livery."

The girl turned back to us. "You'd better know it well — if your friend is guilty of something bad, Sheriff won't dawdle. He'll hang the boy come morning."

I shook her hand quick, knowing we had to find Luke. Feeling the dread in my heart pound like a Cavalry drum in a parade. Walks-Like-a-Feather and I thanked the girl for the information but wasted no more time. We pulled our collars high, held the brims of our hats and dashed out into what had become more snow than rain in an ever-increasing icy cold gale.

We passed a Chinaman's eatery where dead fowl hung to cure beneath a leaky canopy, all of them whipping in the wind. The Chinaman yelled something at us we couldn't understand and began snatching the birds from their hooks so they wouldn't be lost to the storm. The empty frame of a place being built was next, and beyond that a large wooden house, the biggest we'd seen in Ogallala. This posted a sign that read *Board and Rooms for Let.* A hospitable glow filtered through the glass windows and made me wish I was sitting within beside a fire instead of out in such forsaken weather.

By the time we came to a corral and the big barn beside it, my boots were full of cold water.

"Come on," Walks-Like-a-Feather said, and he banged a gloved fist against the small side door to the livery. The wind still blew, but the noise of the rain abated. Big flakes of wet snow and shards of sleet that still stung were what remained. We saw a shadow approach beneath the gap at the base of the entrance. The door cracked enough for a man to eye Walks-Like-a-Feather and me a moment before he beckoned us to come inside where it was surprisingly warmer and cozy.

When my eyes adjusted to the light, I saw we were standing in a smaller space adjacent to the barn proper. A box stove, not unlike Doc Lowry's, kept the place heated. The feller made me think of my pa in the stiff way he moved. Older with a hat but no coat, he wore a sheriff's badge pinned to one of his suspenders. With a gesture, he offered us two empty chairs - part of a circle in front of the stove where him and two other men of about the same age, occupied three more.

"You an Indian?" he asked, sitting before saying anything else.

Walks-Like-a-Feather removed his sombrero and a glove and extended his hand. "My people are Tonkawa. My name is Thomas. Miss Kepler and I come to see about a young friend of ours and our mounts and provisions."

I took off Pa's hat and swished my hair out across one shoulder so they could see I was, in fact, a person of the feminine sort. They all straightened up in their chairs, suddenly putting on airs of a little more formality. The change in their manners didn't make me feel any better about the state of our situation.

"Luke's the lost boy's name," I quickly said between puffs of air to catch my breath. "And there's a donkey too who's mine." I weren't about to go nowhere without either of them.

"Ma'am," the man who'd let us in remarked with a tip of his hat. "Nice to meet you both. My name is Deaver. I am the Sheriff of Ogallala - least as long as the good folks in this town desire it. This gent's my deputy, Caroll Luntz. That man sitting yonder is probably the one you want to speak with."

The third man sort a half stood and touched the brim of his worn, cavalry Stetson. He looked the oldest and had a bushy, overgrown mustache with another hairy tuft below his lower lip. As he moved in the flicker of the fire, I realized his right arm rested in a white cotton sling. The silver circle and star on his coat lapel read *United States Deputy Marshal* in no uncertain terms. He sat back down with a grunt and spoke:

"Only fella I got here is a young man caged in the barn. The boy was tending stolen property and posing as a federal officer of the law."

Stolen property? Only thing that's been stole was all our livestock and the life of my daddy, I thought but did not utter.

"If the boy's name is Luke, that's him," I said. Bolder than perhaps I should've, me lurching to my feet once more, feeling my toes squish against the sodden insides of my boots.

The deputy named Luntz rose, drawing his pistol to counter me with the nervous awkwardness of someone who hadn't done it very often. I raised my hands to where he could see, and Sheriff Deaver placed his over Luntz's revolver to push the barrel down.

"Hold on there, Caroll. These folks just come in out of a storm asking for our help. Let the little lady speak."

The deputy parked his piece back in its holster and sunk again into his chair. The Federal lawman chuckled and watched, but never flinched until he motioned for me to ease myself down as well.

"Lucas Barrientos is my friend, Marshal," I said as I sat again. "He's a Sheriff's Deputy, like Mister Luntz, back in Weld County."

"Weld?"

"Yessir."

"Why is this boy in possession of a government issued horse, rifle and wearing a Federal Officer's identification? Not to mention why are all of you many days ride from your homes in the Colorado Territory?"

I looked at Walks-Like-a-Feather, who lowered his eyes and remained silent, staring at the soles of the other men's shoes.

"I'm waiting," said the marshal with the genesis of impatience in his voice.

"That Winchester and the dapple... they belonged to a man who said he was a Marshal Harry Sturges, sir. I'm the one who rode the horse up here. Luke was federalized and swore an oath to protect the constitution according to Marshal Sturges' wishes. That's why the boy wears the badge."

Deaver, Luntz and that US Marshal all looked at one another.

"You're certain United States Marshal Harry Sturges did this?" said Sheriff Deaver.

"I saw him do it. I swear to you on my pa's grave."

Walks-Like-a-Feather finally spoke. "Her father was murdered ten days back, sir. That is why we come to the State of Nebraska and the town of Ogallala. We trail his killers. And believe this Sturges fellow had something to do with it."

Sheriff Deaver raised his hand, motioning for Walks-Like-a-Feather to pipe down. "Let the girl say her peace. No need to hear your version of the truth yet."

I saw a fire light inside Walks-Like-a-Feather's eyes. "Never you mind," I whispered, not wanting him to get in trouble too. He lowered his gaze to stare at the lawmen's boots again. But I do recall him returning his hat upon his head and slipping his glove back on to cover his bare hand in that same moment.

"And where is this Harry Sturges now, Miss... what is your name again?" the deputy marshal asked.

"Kepler... Mae Kepler," I quick replied, knowing my heart skipped a beat and began pitter-pattering like a jack rabbit on the chopping block. I swallowed, fearing I was about to end my own life revealing what I was about to reveal. "I done it sir. A half-day's ride north of Jacob's Ferry. I shot and killed Harry Sturges after I found he was involved in the killing of my pa."

All of them started laughing.

"You killed a Federal Marshal?" asked Sheriff Deaver and he guffawed a few more times. "A girl as petite as you... And you are certain of this?"

"How old are you, darlin'?" Deputy Luntz asked, leaning forward, staring. Laughing a little less now. I knew I didn't like him. Nor did I like how he was drinking in the appearance of my hair and face on down to my boots.

"Enough of this."

The deputy marshal stood and straightened his coat. The other two mimicked him, Sheriff Deaver putting on his. "They can share the cage with the boy. We'll telegraph the judge in the morning. See if he wants to set a trial or be done with it and hang all three by day's end."

"Hang? Wait... what?" I said, suddenly feeling all sweaty, hearing my heart now thump like a runaway train. "My friend here didn't do anything. Luke neither. They been helping me locate these fugitives." I began to shiver as I stood trying to protest what that marshal was saying. Felt myself wobble even as I forced my hand to move slowly toward the upper edge of Pa's coat pocket.

Walks-Like-a-Feather's fingers got there first.

His hand slipped inside and withdrew the Colt. Then he pointed the piece at Deputy Luntz. "No offense intended, but I'll not spend another night in a white man's jail cell. Nor will I hang for something I did not do."

Walks-Like-A-Feather backed out of the circle of chairs with the ease of a barn cat. Kept the pistol trained on the three Lawmen until his form blended into the shadows. Luntz took the chance, jerked his gun and fired a shot as the Tonkawa escaped through the door, calling to me from the darkness beyond. "Don't worry, Mae Kepler... Heed your instincts!"

Another voice spoke from somewhere inside the big part of the livery. This one also familiar.

"Mae! Is that you? You alright?"

"Luke!" I started to answer, but Deaver and Luntz held me. Told me to speak no more.

The marshal pulled his own weapon and rushed to the door where he found no blood and nothing worth chasing. No clear footprints were in the fresh snow, nor any other visible sign Walks-Like-a-Feather had ever been there.

"Indians behave like they are creatures not of this earth sometimes," the marshal grumbled after he barred the door again. "No matter. We'll see about him in the morning."

He told them others to release me. And guided me by my elbow through the livery to where Luke sat in a simple chamber encased in iron bars about the floor, the four walls, and on top near the rafters above. Carroll Luntz made me take off my boots and checked my coat and clothing for anything else that might be considered dangerous. His hands took extra time, making certain nothing was hidden beneath my blouse or tucked below the waist of Ma's riding pants.

I hugged Luke when the sheriff got me inside the cage. He passed us two blankets and a canteen of water and locked the door again. "No shenanigans this night and Deputy Luntz will feed you both an egg and a biscuit when he rises."

"Don't you men believe me?" I asked in desperation, wondering what was to become of us. "I killed that man, it's true. But it was because of what he and them others conspired to do to my pa. The feller at the Café beside Jacob's Ferry told me Harry Sturges weren't no real lawman. Just pretending to be one. I guess I still don't know what the truth is and what ain't."

"I believe something happened, Mae Kepler," said the marshal. "Might be murder. Might not. None of it sounds good."

"I was there, Marshal, sir," Luke said. "That man, whoever he was, he stabbed Mae and would have finished me if she hadn't shot him in the head. Blew his top clear off.

"I promise we'll revisit your stories in the morning after I inquire with the judge," continued the marshal. "The truth has a way of getting all tangled - especially late in the night. I *can* tell you three facts that I have no doubt about as they relate to your deposition. And any person here in Ogallala will voucher them true.

"I am United States Deputy Marshal Harry Sturges. I still possess the crown of my skull and do believe I am still breathing.

I expect we'll uncover the remaining veracity of these matters come daybreak."

CHAPTER 18

LUKE TOOK MY face in his hands and kissed me inside that dark cell after the lawmen disappeared. He didn't do it straight off. Took hold of me first; me shaking like a leaf from thinking about how them officers were planning a hanging without no proper discussion or trial. I mean, I never heard of a judge deciding someone's fate across so many miles on an electric wire.

Luke didn't try to put his hands where they didn't belong. He whispered in my ear telling me not to worry. "Everything is going to be fine. We'll figure this out." Then he leaned in and did the deed. Mashed his mouth on mine as if it would help.

Now I don't want to pretend I didn't feel something. Something nice. Luke's lips on mine were warm and soft and somehow sweet. But the marshal said we'd hang, and my mind was going like a runaway coach on a narrow road. *Figure it out* was all I wanted to do. Ponder and discuss our options to make some sort of plan. The peril of our situation didn't look to me like it was about to turn out all fine and dandy because Luke said it would be so.

So, I pushed the boy away and sat on a pile of hay in the middle of that locked iron cage – annoyed with him and worried I was about to be hung for killing a man I didn't know like I thought I knew. A dead man who may or may not have really been involved with the murder of my pa and attack on my ma. Fact of the matter was, I pulled first and shot, though nothing happened. Sturges stabbed me, beat on Luke and I shot him dead on the second try. Is that fair and square, or did that make me a murderer in the eyes of God and the law?

I did not know.

"Maybe if I explained things better?" I finally whispered to Luke.

"Sorry I kissed you."

"Stop worrying about kissing and such, Lucas Barrientos. We need to think on how to improve our situation." Though I admit the notion of him kissing me was still harboring about in my mind. Me conjuring up an image of Ma and thinking on what she might say regarding such a thing... If I ever had to chance to tell her.

"We explained to them what happened, Mae. Didn't we?" he whispered back.

"Oh, shush."

I let the episode with the three lawmen rattle around in my head a few more moments. Luke wasn't entirely right. My explanations were muddled and mixed even though we told them officers most of what we knew.

"Maybe it's because I was nervous." I said, breaking the silence again. "Our story came out all hurly-burly. In bits and pieces and in no suitable order."

The livery was mostly quiet when I paused to stew again. It smelled of hay and manure, making me worry about Robert as I heard all them horses down the line shift in their stalls a little while they slept. Their puffing and breathing sounded slow and steady and relaxed.

After a time, Luke's breath grew regular as well. My shoulders felt heavy. I caught myself nodding off when there was a knock on the small door at the far end of the big barn. Even though we were right next to one another I couldn't see Luke - only feel his presence next to mine. It was very early before dawn, so I took his hand in mine to rouse him.

"That you, Sheriff?" a voice asked. Carroll Luntz must have

taken on the job of guarding us for the balance of the night. The deputy lit a lantern on a small table and I could just make him out across the big barn moving to that side door. When he opened it, I witnessed a shadow of movement. Heard a thud and a scuffle and Luntz wheezing in a bruised voice, "Please don't."

His words quickly ended with a grunt.

The rumpus woke the horses. One kicked against a stall door, and this set off all the others, who moved about nervously in their stalls. A bridle tinkled as it dangled from a hook somewhere. There were a few stomps of hooves.

And a nicker.

Luke squeezed my fingers to tell me he was awake. Then he and I began to hear the scrapes of metal and the splintering of wood. A set of keys rattled and moments later, the glow of a lantern approached, bringing Walks-Like-a-Feather with it like an apparition beside our cell. He released us using an iron key and a turn of the lock.

"Saddle the horses and get your burro," he whispered. "I'll recover our guns and provisions."

"You didn't kill that man, did you?" I said.

He handed Luke the lantern and took my hands in his. Set a soft pair of buckskin gloves in them for me to take. "Deputy Luntz will have a lump on his head when he wakes. Nothing worse. We'll lock him in his own jail cell before we're gone." Walks-Like-a-Feather stepped away, disappearing into the darkness again to find our things.

In haste, I dropped my feet in my damp boots that were still setting outside the cage. Got Pa's hat and gave Luke his as well, then put on them fancy gloves. We passed the line of horses in stalls being boarded by their owners. Our stock was near the back of the barn and seemed a little prickly like the rest. The dapple and my Robert stood in one. Luke's bay and Walks-Like-a-Feather's gray stallion were next door.

Of course, Robert lit up as soon as he saw me. He nuzzled and blew snot out his nostrils across the backs of my clean gloves. I expect that was a donkey's way of saying how-do. I gave him a hug around his neck and a scratch behind the ears. He pushed closer against me, enjoying the warmth of my arms about him.

Robert seemed content enough sharing space with that dapple, having spent so many hours being tethered to him on our ride north.

"Should we leave the marshal his belongings?" I asked Luke as he wrestled to get his kit squared on his bay. "I mean... I could saddle Robert. Or double with you on yours."

"Put your gear on the dapple," he said after a pause. "It is what Thomas wanted."

"You could take mine," a small voice interrupted from out of the gloom.

Luke spun, cocked his fist back to take a swing at the young girl who'd snuck up behind us. I took a step away, holding Robert tight. But he only snorted as donkeys do and didn't seem disturbed by the newcomer's presence.

"And you might be?" Luke said, still ready to take a poke.

That's when I realized I'd seen her before. "You... you were the one who prodded me in the back at the saloon," I said, putting my hand on top of Luke's to keep his fist contained. "This girl told me and Thomas where to find you."

"Evy Guntersen," she said, a twinkle in them bright eyes of hers. "That is my given name."

Luke let me ease his fist down.

"And I ain't no bar whore if that's what you two are thinking."

"We...," Luke fumbled his words before glancing at me and then back again at Evy Guntersen. "Neither of us would believe that," he finally declared. "Besides, you must be too young for such a thing."

"Old enough," Evy Guntersen spoke right back. "I've done what needs doing. And I sure as hell bet I can ride and shoot better than the likes of you."

There was a bit of silence in that big barn until I started chuckling. Evy Guntersen must've liked that. Her face softened and she smiled. "Like I was trying to tell you, I got two saddle horses I might let you borrow. Long as you pledge to take me with."

"Why are you here... in this livery, Miss Evy Guntersen?" I said.

"This is where I keep my bed. My uncle, he owns the place."

"And you waited all this time to show yourself?" said Luke.

"Not like you were about to leave anywhere this night, being all locked up like you was. Besides I wanted to make sure you and her were honest folk. When the Indian come back, I figured I'd make my move."

"Guess we passed the test," said Luke.

"Well, I've been listening. Heard your stories and what them lawmen were saying. I know it's true you killed someone, Miss Mae Kepler."

Her words drew the hurt of my past into the present. Made me want to look away. My eyes drifted down to search for the tips of my boots in the dim lantern light. But Evy Guntersen extended a gentle hand to me, took mine in hers.

"Pleased to meet you by the way," she said. "Formally that is. It's clear as day to me the only witnesses yet alive are declaring you killed that man to defend yourself and the memory of your pa. I don't know the marshal as well because he's only here now and again. But Deaver and Luntz aren't worth the salt they're made of. Least that's what my uncle says. If you want to live, we best be on our way."

"What about your uncle?" I said.

"What about him?"

"Won't he be angry?"

Walks-Like-a-Feather came up behind the girl before she could answer. "You are a quiet one, aren't you?" he whispered.

Evy turned and looked at him. "I can be if it's required." Her teeth showed in the shape of a full grin this time through the dim light. "Like I said, I can shoot too. Got me a forty-four caliber Henry Rifle."

"1860?" asked Luke.

The girl nodded.

She was definitely younger than me, but pretty. I liked the way the light from the glow of the lantern danced in her eyes and across her slim form. I could tell Luke was thinking much the same, the way his gaze stayed with her as she moved. Not sure I was very happy about that.

"Well, Evy Guntersen," said Walks-Like-a-Feather. "If you want out of here, we are leaving soon as you saddle those horses of yours." He reached his hand out to shake hers. "Looks like you've become our newest member."

"You mean like... like in a gang of robbers?"

"Outlaws to some. Mostly we're a bunch of meandering misfits," I said, shaking the girl's hand once more, this time judging the strength of her grasp. "Ain't that right, Thomas?"

It was Walks-Like-a-Feather's turn to reveal his pearly whites.

We left everything we believed belonged to Marshal Sturges. The real one. I prayed the gesture might help wipe our slate clean. Clean except for maybe that part about me killing a man. We set it all in the stall with the big dapple, who didn't seem to mind us leaving him anyhow. The Winchester and the twin pistol rig that had been put away since that night by the campfire. We also left the bedroll and slicker, and the pepper grinder too. I didn't abandon the spyglass though. Kept that in one of the packs strapped across Robert's hide because I wasn't convinced it had ever belonged to the marshal and knew we might need it before our intended task was complete.

We saddled Luke's bay, Walks-Like-a-Feather's stallion, and the two horses Evy Guntersen avowed were hers. I tied Robert to the one I was to ride and glanced at Evy. She looked ready enough, wearing calf-high boots, dungarees, riding coat and a flop hat. Brought along her Henry repeater, a pocket full of cartridges and the bedding she'd used in her bunk at the livery.

As Evy led us out the rear doors of the livery, Luke leaned off his saddle towards me and whispered: "Why do you think she wants to go?"

"I don't particularly care," I replied. "The girl's got the mounts we need and another rifle she insists she can use. We can fret over the details of her feelings after we put some distance between us and the law in this town."

111

CHAPTER 19

BEFORE DAWN, we followed Evy Guntersen through the corral and I could tell right away she was comfortable in a saddle. The girl rode her mount with ease through pasture gates and across slippery, snow-covered fields. That horse minded her well. She took us east for a mile or more and in the dim light, we finally saw the water tank silhouetted against the sky just like the barkeep at *Aufdengarten* had described. The grange, corral and a cattle chute were there too, sandwiched between the road east and the train tracks that paralleled it.

Evy slowed to let us bunch around her.

"The stockman who runs the grange knows me because of my uncle. He uses our corral to stage livestock for sale most weeks. I'll introduce you if he's there. Man drinks a lot of coffee so we might bum a hot cup off him."

She rode towards the lengthy low building, and we followed again.

"You think it's safe to trust this girl's judgement?" I asked Walks-Like-a-Feather, thinking on Luke's words earlier.

"Why? Because Miss Guntersen is younger than you?"

I hesitated a reply. Looking at the girl again, trying to get a better hold on what I truly thought of her disposition. "She can't be more than eleven or twelve, don't you think?" I asked.

"Same as the girl who schooled me to ride hideaway style... whose lessons, through me, taught you much the same. Wisdom and the passage of time don't always walk hand in hand, Mae Kepler."

Evy, who still rode with poise in her saddle, turned back as we watched her, looking at us with a cheerful smile and those eyes, encouraging each of us to keep up the brisk pace she set. There weren't no denying Walks-Like-a-Feather's observation. Our new companion possessed a natural charm we each felt obliged to follow.

By the time we crossed the last fallow field, the sky was brightening as it does on a clear day before sunrise and reflected off the fresh snow. The grange was not much more than a long roof of sorts. Mostly open to the weather allowing buyers to view what men brought to sell.

A fellow wearing a Bollman hat and a cowhide coat stood at a stone fire pit nestled beside the building. Like Evy had predicted, the man was watching a big old kettle brew as it hung hot above the blaze. We could smell a broad skillet of biscuits that browned beside it as well.

"Evy Guntersen! What on earth are you doing out here at this forsaken hour?"

She dismounted and ran to the man. The two hugged and Evy waved us in to join them. "These folks been boarding at the livery. I told 'em I'd bring them to you because they're searching for some drovers who might be trying to sell stolen cattle."

"Well, come on. Warm yourselves. Got coffee and a biscuit if you'd care. Let's find out if I'm the man to help."

Luke dismounted first. Boy was already eyeing them hot rolls in that skillet. Walks-Like-a-Feather didn't move. Looking uncomfortable, he scanned the ground from his saddle on back towards town. I swung my leg over and dropped beside the gelding I'd borrowed. "Evy Guntersen, this animal of yours have a name? He's mighty easy."

She grinned, showing her teeth again. "That one's Midas. He's a good-natured horse. The other's Max. They share the same momma."

"Thanks for letting me borrow him this day."

The stockman observed the exchange between me and the girl but said nothing.

"You gonna get down, Thomas?" I asked, but he still didn't move.

"*Haáahe*, friend. Please do," said the stockman gesturing for Walks-Like-a-Feather to step down. "Come to the fire. It is good for warming the soul of any man…" He turned to Evy, "Or woman."

I believe she liked that.

"Corral the horses under the roof. It's empty. I've nothing for sale at this hour yet."

Walks-Like-a-Feather looked again towards town, before finally dismounting. "You speak the Cheyenne?" he asked, leading his gray behind him to the fire.

The stockman looked slightly embarrassed. "Nah, I've picked up morsels here and there. This endeavor brings many folks to Ogallala. Knowing a bit of a man's tongue brings a better price and many a contented partner in business."

"And life," agreed Walks-Like-a-Feather.

The man in the Bollman bared his hand, reaching to shake. "Name's Josiah Thorndike." Walks-Like-a-Feather shook first. Luke and I each took it in turn, introducing ourselves as well. Mister Thorndike's grip was firm and spirited. He held my hand a little longer than the others. "You're cut from much the same cloth as Evy here, aren't you, young lady? A little older, I expect. And I'll wager you shoot as well as you ride too, Miss Kepler."

I looked at Evy, who gazed back like she was now sizing *me* up.

"Thomas here is teaching me how to handle a long rifle. My daddy showed me to hunt birds, varmints and such with a 12-gauge." I thought of Pa keeping my arm straight at the elbow with his large hand. Me holding the shotgun as level as I could while aiming at a short pyramid of stones he'd piled for me to shoot apart. The memory frittered away when the sounds of cattle and their drovers approaching filled my ears. The sun crested at the horizon, giving the snow a fresh brilliance and starting the clock on a new day.

I gave Evy a nervous eye, knowing a lot of new faces would soon arrive and that we, most certainly, were still wanted by the law.

"Mister Thorndike," she said. "These people don't have much time."

"Train to catch?"

When none of us laughed, Walks-Like-a-Feather chimed in, explaining what had happened to Pa and Ma and the animals that had been rustled from our farm.

Thorndike turned serious. "I apologize for making light of your situation, Miss Kepler. A man named Jim Butler is coming in as we speak. I made this coffee and biscuits for him and his boys, although I've been happy to share with you folks as well. Jim Butler's been leading cattle drives since '67. He knows many a fellow trail boss and what they might be planning."

We thawed some of the chill of the morning with steaming coffee and each ate a biscuit by the time this feller Jim Butler and his men brought their cattle in close. Introductions were made over the noise of his excited herd while Butler's riders worked them longhorns into the transfer corral behind the chute. I gave him a description of Little John and what he and his associates done.

Jim Butler was a black man, younger than Mister Coates. More rugged and striking. He took a sip of coffee, and I noticed how Butler's eyes returned to Walks-Like-a-Feather several times, while he warmed his hands on the metal cup. "It's late in the season. All of us been pushing luck to beat this snow, so not many left out there. I do know of two more small herds forming to the south. But those are good men bringing 'em in. Not the type to steal." Jim Butler turned and shouted at one of his boys who approached on a pretty appaloosa. "Hey Josey, didn't you bump into a wrangler camped right close to our herd a couple of days back?"

"Yeah, Boss."

The young drover pivoted in his saddle and pointed back to where they'd brought their cattle across the road. "Fella is camped three and a half, maybe four miles yonder watching two dozen horses. Had a mixed herd of mostly short horns with him.

115

Even had a score or more of milk cows. That's why I told you about it, Mister Butler. Fellow was a bit queer. All jittery when he spoke. Said they'd come up from the Territory and were looking for buyers."

"How big was the crew?"

"Seemed small. Some had gone into town I expect. We saw three swing riders minding the herd. Might have been a drag man farther out we didn't see."

"What was the wrangler's name?" Jim Butler asked.

"Francis."

CHAPTER 20

MY THROAT WENT all tight when I heard the name, knowing he was one who harmed my ma. Luke dumped the dregs of his coffee on the frozen ground, noticing me and then nervously glancing back across the fields towards Ogallala. "Mae, we should go. The sun's up and we've gotten what we need to find this perpetrator." He avoided Thorndike, only looking at Walks-Like-a-Feather and me.

"The deputy's right," agreed Walks-Like-a-Feather. "We should be out of Mister Thorndike's way so he can get on with his business."

"Deputy?" said Thorndike to grab Luke's attention. "Barrientos, isn't it? Where's your badge?"

Luke's shoulders slumped beneath his Mackinaw long coat, suddenly seeming unsure and a little humiliated, knowing the real Marshal Sturges had unpinned his star. "I... I'm trying not to peddle the fact too much, if you know what I mean. Especially doing what we're doing. It's a dangerous undertaking, chasing fugitives."

"He's under my employ," I said to try and set things straight again. "Thomas too."

Luke excused himself and moved towards our horses while I grabbed cups from everyone and set them in the wash pail near the fire. "Evy, go with Luke to retrieve the animals," I said. "Sounds like we have an appointment to visit with a man named

117

Francis."

"Yes, ma'am!"

They hustled to gather our mounts, and my donkey. I shook hands with Thorndike and Jim Butler, again, thanking them for their help and kindness. Once we were all in the saddle, the young drover named Josey offered to ride with us on his appaloosa to the road and south for a short distance to get us headed on a proper course.

"Follow the mark of the herd. They'll lead you most of the way to that outfit's camp," Josey said. He turned to ride back for the grange but stopped a few strides out, spinning that pretty horse about before we completely parted ways. "Miss Kepler, I do hope we meet again. You and your friends be careful when you tangle with that Francis. He was a peculiar sort of man."

I could tell Luke was watching as Josey rode off. Walks-Like-a-Feather broke the boy's concentration when he told him to get on with things and lead. Me, my donkey, and Evy strung along behind him. Walks-Like-a-Feather pushed from the rear. He said it was good we were following the trampled earth and snow turned by Jim Butler's herd because it would help hide our intentions.

"Ride with purpose this morning. Don't be lulled by the peaceful nature of the land out here," he warned. "The Ogallala lawmen will be on our tails if they aren't already. And the men we seek will kill us before they'll ever let us bring them in."

"Trouble ahead and trouble behind," Luke said with a nudge against his bay's flank to get her trotting faster. He kept us at that brisk pace for two miles until we came to a shallow crick and halted at its edge. Walks-Like-a-Feather decided we should leave the broad trail left by the herd. He had us swing to follow the crick's flow upstream for a hundred yards until he was satisfied we'd gone enough to mask the change. He directed Luke to turn south again, up and through a patch of snow-covered junipers.

On the higher ground, Walks-Like-a-Feather instructed us again: "Remain low in the saddle. Keep to the scrub. Let your horse lead to find the best paths and maybe we'll purchase a little more time to do what we need to do when we meet our man."

Evy and I rode in the middle again and she asked what the

deal was about my donkey. "Robert's all I got left from our farm. I wear my pa's coat and hat, and Ma's buckskin trousers. So, I'm always keeping their memories close." I looked at my donkey and recalled the cold afternoon I'd ridden Janey out of our barn and found him wandering near the road. Leaving Mister Coates alone to bury Pa and care for my ma.

I smiled at Evy. "Robert's like a familiar friend. He stinks pretty bad and can be ornery, but he's good company most of the time."

"How about Deputy Barrientos?" she asked, me suddenly feeling a little wary when she did. "Ain't he from where you grew up? Seems like a nice enough young man." Luke was trotting just ahead of us on his bay.

"Oh, he is nice. Although I'm not sure Luke's yet a man and I've only known him since my family was attacked coming on two weeks now. Circumstances brought him to me or me to him. He's not from Weld County, though. His kin live down New Mexico way."

"Mesilla," Luke chimed in, slowing his bay to talk. "And you should be calling me, Luke, Miss Evy Guntersen." His horse fell in with our two as he continued to chatter: "The marshal took my badge so I'm not sure how much of a deputy I am anymore."

She flashed those eyes and he smiled right back. "Like Mae says, my mama and pop live in Mesilla. Grands too. The Sheriff back in Weld is an old friend of my father's." He edged his horse close to mine so he could take my hand as we rode side by side.

"He's good at butting in, ain't he?" I said, squeezing his, wanting him to know I was only teasing.

Evy watched us ride a minute or two. "You two courting?" she asked, reeling in our attention again.

"Me and Mae?" Luke said, releasing my hand, tipping the brim of his hat towards me. "Better you pose that question to the lady... I just do what she tells."

"I haven't fully decided yet." I gave Luke and her a sideways grin and spurred my horse to canter ahead of both of theirs. "Despite all his chattering, and them big ears he possesses... the boy does work hard to make it so," I called over my shoulder as I took the lead.

"My ears are not so big! They frame my sweet face and keep my hat from sliding down to the bridge of my nose."

Evy laughed, enjoying our banter. I heard Thomas chuckle from behind — the Tonkawa humored by our discussions as well.

"What about you, Miss Guntersen?" Luke asked. "Why does a young girl such as yourself want to leave her home with a bunch of folks, who, it would seem, are now on the run from the law? This one especially," he said.

"That boy pointing at me, Evy?" I asked.

"Finger aimed right at you, ma'am," she confirmed with a laugh.

Course I slowed the horse I was riding to a shuffle so I could hear how the girl might respond to Luke's question. Evy Guntersen looked at me and then back at Walks-Like-a-Feather before she spoke.

"Well, I know I'm petite, but I am fully thirteen, a fact you should know, Deputy Barrientos. Ogallala ain't my home, and, although my uncle took me in, he ain't exactly the kind you want to spend a lot of alone time with."

"He mistreat you?" said Luke, keeping his horse loping beside hers.

"Gave me a roof over my head and food to eat. Pays me a little coin for the many things I do. But I done plenty and when I heard yours and Mae's story, I believed it was a sign for me to chance something new. If not better, perhaps riding with you folks will prove yet to be much more interesting."

The horses balked as we skirted around a stretch of prickly thickets and then coaxed them up a slope of snow and loose scree. We settled again into a steady pace after, and I slowed Midas back beside Max to see Evy saddled on him with a fresh set of eyes. "What happened to your parents? If you don't mind my prying?"

"Ma died at my birth. Pa was slain by Comanche two years back on the trail from Tucson. Least that's what the Army captain said who brought daddy home in a pine box."

Walks-Like-a-Feather urged his gray to catch us when he heard that part. Evy acknowledged his gaze and waved her hand.

"Weren't your fault, Mister Thomas. I know you come from a different people. There are good and bad seeds everywhere. Folks have reasons and purposes for doing what's done. My pa taught me to never hold no grudges." She looked at him again. "Though sometimes such expectations are easier spoken than met."

Walks-Like-a-Feather seemed to accept her words as sincere and eased his horse back to mind the trail we were leaving behind again.

"Well, I thank you for coming with," I said. "And letting me ride atop Midas. He is a good horse and far better than me having to saddle Robert or being stuck with *that* boy on his bay."

Luke gave me a wink, making me happy he'd come into my life. And even though we just met, I was beginning to feel the same about Evy Guntersen too.

We quieted for a time, knowing we were getting near. At the third mile, we began to hear strange sounds, surfacing in and out of the breeze. Almost like a moaning. The noises slowly shaped into a melody of sorts, and we realized it was a voice coming from the throat of a man doing his best to carry a tune.

"Whoa, there," I told Midas and slung myself down into the snow. Drawing my Robert to me with his line, I dug in his packs to find the spyglass. "Keep the horses settled until I call for you," I whispered. Evy dismounted and took Midas' and Max's reins as I moved on foot up to the top of the next rise, motioning for Walks-Like-a-Feather and Luke to join me. The three of us hugged the cold ground and crawled to where we might see who was making all the racket.

I stretched out the telescope to its full length, propped the device on a rock and peered through its eyepiece. With a twist and turn or two for adjustment I focused on something I didn't quite expect. A man was standing out there in a bare patch beside a chuck wagon, brushing the hairs on the flank of a horse and swinging his hips while he belted out a sorry old tune at the top of his lungs:

Oh, I ain't got noooo father.
I ain't got noooo mother,

121

My friends, they all left me when first I did roam.

My face must have shown a little wonder. Luke pried the glass out of my hands to see for himself what I was peering at. "It's a solitary man... and he's singing badly," Luke whispered, letting loose a soft laugh. "Okay, the fella's now doing a twirl like he's at a dance. Brushing the horse in between at the same time."

Ohhhh... I ain't got noooo sister.
I ain't got noooo brother,

Before the man finished his jig, Luke passed the glass to Walks-Like-a-Feather.

I'm a poor lonesome cowboy a long ways from home...

"Is that your Francis?" he asked quietly after pulling the spyglass from his eye.

I shrugged my shoulders. "I was hog tied in the back of our wagon. Never actually *seen* Francis nor the other named Frank. Just heard them complain to the big feller with the beard."

"Little John," whispered Luke.

"Yep."

"Do you see anyone else?" asked Luke as Walks-Like-a-Feather continued to survey the campsite. He collapsed the telescope, gave it back to me, and told us we best be getting our guns. "That fellow appears to be alone except for a cavvy of six horses picketed farther back. Maybe the others did take the herd in to sell like Jim Butler's young drover supposed."

Walks-Like-a-Feather led us off the rise but continued to speak with a quiet voice. "I don't know how good a shot Miss Guntersen is, but she and I are going to cover you with the long guns from this ridge here and the one west, across the way. The Army calls this type of arrangement a crossfire. It should give us an upper hand – if none of our singing wrangler's associates return."

Luke and I gazed at each other. "What are me and him supposed to do?"

"Go meet the man, Mae Kepler… and do what we come thus far to do."

We scrambled on down to where Evy was waiting with the horses and my donkey. Luke put extra .44 rounds in the pocket of his Mackinaw and checked the load of the pistol tied to the pommel of his saddle making sure it was ready. I released the cylinder on the 1848, seeing that the cap and ball were still packed proper. *You got four shots,* I reminded myself. *Don't waste none in haste.*

Walks-Like-a-Feather whispered to Evy what he wanted. She tied Max to the lower branches of a small juniper and ran to the rise we'd just left clutching her Henry and looking mighty severe. Walks-Like-a Feather took hold of my donkey's and his horse's leads. "Count to thirty, then move in on that fellow. See what he has to say for himself." He swung west, running low, to set himself on the next hillock, covering our approach and completing the crossfire.

Luke leaned in against me while we stood beside our horses, each keeping them still. "You do know your numbers to thirty?" he whispered.

"Shush," I said, straightening the collar of his coat. I pushed his bangs back under his hat with the tips of my fingers, took off Pa's Slouch, and kissed him before I proceeded to counting. By the time I got to twenty-five, my hat was back on my head. We both saddled and broke for a gap in the rise between us and the singing cowboy. The cleft was icy in the shadowed parts, and muddy where the sun had softened the frozen ground. The man saw us and stopped what he was doing as soon as we parted the scrub and rode into the clear.

"Morning friend," Luke called. Feller dropped the horse-brush he'd been using and scrambled to snatch a Winchester leaned against the tongue of the chuck wagon. He levered a round into the repeater and pointed its muzzle in our direction.

"I ain't your friend, Mister," he yelled back. The weasel's squeaky voice was etched in my brain, only having heard it but once or twice before. *Speak for yerself, Little John.*

I heard again the pain in my ma's voice when she'd called my name. Me still hog-tied in our wagon with no ability to help. I

123

tamped down the rage once more that still dwelled in my heart as Luke and I reined our horses to a halt not thirty feet from where the man stood pointing his rifle.

"Just trying to be neighborly," said Luke.

"I ain't your neighbor neither."

"Well, actually you are," Luke said. He turned in his saddle and pointed north, leading the man to ease off a little and to gaze in the same direction as well. The barrel of his Winchester descended, and I slipped my hand in Pa's coat pocket to take hold of the Army Dragoon.

"My group brought in a small mixed herd last night," Luke continued like he was just gabbing. "We are a mile yonder. Fellow named Josey told us to find a trail boss who goes by Little John. Said he might be able to help us sell our stake."

"Mixed? Stole them cows, didn't you?" the man invited, lowering his rifle at the ground a few inches more.

"Let's just say they've been branded fresh and are ready to move."

The man laughed. "Little John. He ain't no trail boss but knows a thing or two about selling what needs to be sold quick."

I couldn't wait no more.

"Your name Francis?" I said, and slowly removed Pa's hat with my left hand. Shook my hair loose, using the brim to hide the fact that my other hand was shoved deep in my pocket. "I believe we've met before."

"A woman? Well, looky here, we got us a cowgirl." He ignored me and my words, speaking only to Luke. "I bet you been riding that one a few miles each night. Maybe I can give her a whirl if we come to terms? Sort of a side deal Little John need not know about."

By the time Francis looked back at me I'd drawn the Dragoon and set the hammer. He smiled, his eyes on the pistol, and finally answered my question. "No ma'am, I don't recall you. I'd remember a woman with a big old gun like that."

He flinched to raise the Winchester. Before I knew to shoot, Luke jerked his peacemaker out of the holster at his saddle and fired. His bullet struck Francis in the arm balancing the repeater. Another struck him low in the flank from the opposite direction.

That one went right on through and we heard a crack from the ridge where Walks-Like-a-Feather was perched. I wound up shooting what was left of the man in the leg.

His Winchester clattered on the ground and Francis collapsed cussing and hollering. He looked at his shattered arm and then at his other hand which he clutched against the hole in his side. "I'm bleeding," he sputtered. Luke dismounted still aiming his forty-four. I did the same, running to the man. Fury, fear, and remorse swirling about in my head.

"Please don't die," I said crouching. Wanting to hear why he'd done what he'd done and confused about how I felt watching blood flow from this terrible man.

"I'm dead already," he told me like he knew it was true.

"My name's Mae Kepler. I need you to know who I am," I said as I stuffed the big Dragoon back down into Pa's coat pocket. "Your boss Little John killed my daddy. I believe you and that other feller named Frank violated and shot my ma in our home ten days back."

He coughed and looked upon me again. "You're the girl John left in the wagon," Francis sputtered through a laugh. "Guess you done young Bobcat before Bobcat could do you."

The memory of the boy peering at me over the side of our wagon and Mister Coates sticking a knife in his throat flooded my brain. "Weren't no doing involved. Only killing," I said and stood, no longer wanting to remember anything about this scoundrel.

"Your friends... they in town?" Luke said in his ear.

"Little John... he'll track all of you down," Francis coughed. There was blood now inside his mouth. It ran, dripping through the stubble on his chin onto the bib of his coat. "Ain't gonna get far."

Francis quieted a moment, then sighed long like a pig bladder losing air and perished with his eyes open.

CHAPTER 21

"WHAT DO WE DO?" I asked, looking at the lifeless man on the ground. Luke stood, stuffing his peacemaker in the waist of his trousers. He picked up the Winchester and gave it to me – a "yellow boy" carbine like the one the marshal had kept. The rifle felt easy in my hands, with the graceful curve of its brass receiver and the weight of its smooth, stout walnut stock. Then Luke began going through Francis' pockets.

"Should we be doing that to a dead man?"

"A good detective always investigates the details, Mae. That's what Sheriff Conley says. Don't you want to know what he's carrying?" He nodded towards the Chuck Wagon. "We'll go through that quick too. Before his friends return."

"But isn't this thieving?"

"We haven't taken anything yet, Mae. And besides, you didn't seem to have a problem with it the first time we employed someone else's belongings."

I must have looked pained as I recalled the crackle and dim flicker of a small campfire and the flash of the dragoon I'd triggered to kill the imposter Harry Sturges.

"It's alright, Mae. We've only done what we had to do. And right now, we at least need to find something to eat. The food we packed is all but gone, and we gave most of the antelope you

126

shot to the Cheyenne." Luke's eyes surveyed the dead wrangler's campsite once more and returned to mine. "Ogallala is no longer an option for groceries anytime soon. So, we need to see what we can scavenge."

I took a step back, knowing he was right, but suddenly worried about Evy and Walks-Like-a-Feather. The girl was waiting at her same spot on the ridge north and waved when she saw me looking. The Tonkawa had already ventured most of the way down from his place on the other rise, leading the gray and my donkey to join us.

"Stay up there, Evy. You're the lookout!" I shouted, and she acknowledged me a second time.

"This anyone you know?" Luke asked, drawing my attention back to him as he crouched over the dead outlaw's form. He passed me a small bit of stiff cardboard, which I took, and to my astonishment, saw my ma and pa staring back at me from the small oval.

Young and determined. Handsome and beautiful.

I began to cry.

"What's wrong?"

Through my tears I told him about the locket Pa had purchased the morning he'd been murdered. The same one Little John stole. Luke took me in his arms while I cried a little longer. His embrace drew more memories out of me — my last morning with Pa, standing in the street in front of the mercantile back in Weld. I felt the ache inside my soul rise again. The ache of loss and of not knowing if my ma were yet alive.

"You sure there was nothing else on Francis?" I asked.

"Only the photograph and four bits in his left pocket which I did not take. My guess is Little John traded your family's locket and chain for cash money."

Walks-Like-a-Feather arrived putting his arms around both of us. He gave me a kerchief to dab my eyes, and I showed him the photograph as well.

The Tonkawa smiled, touching my parents' faces with his finger. Much like I'd done the first time Pa showed me.

"Plain as day, I see you in them, Mae Kepler," he said. "It's good to finally gaze upon your kin. Even if it is through a picture on such a tiny piece of paper." When he handed it back to me with care, Walks-Like-a-Feather took my hand in his. "I have witnessed them in you as well. Miss Mae, you are a decent woman. And this truth is why I am here now helping you and the boy pursue these beasts."

"You're gonna make me cry again, Thomas."

"It is good to shed tears for the ones we love. But we haven't such luxury right now. It's time to prepare with haste before this outfit returns to discover what we've done."

He and Luke hurried to the Chuck Wagon to search for things we might need. Quick to gather salt pork, cornmeal, and lard from the chuck box, and cartridges for the Winchester. In back they found blankets, a tarp, and some cord to use as a shelter against the weather next time we camped.

I clenched my eyes closed for a moment and took a deep breath, knowing I needed to help. Luke found the scabbard for the Winchester and gave me the ammunition he'd discovered. I put a dozen more of the .44 rimfires in my pocket and slipped the rest in one of my saddlebags. Then tied the scabbard and rifle to my rig on Midas. "I'll check them horses," I said, and ran to see about the ones Walks-Like-a-Feather had spied farther out.

There were six steeds picketed in a grass patch two hundred feet back. They began to fidget as I came close. Simple horses, dark brown, and charcoal, that looked tired and thin from the drive north. These were part of the saddle band the drovers used as spare mounts to rotate through each day. It was a wrangler's job to care for them during a drive. Horses couldn't last for so long under a saddle from camp to camp. The cavvy of extras let each animal take turns being ridden and resting and then being ridden again without injury for many days on end.

With twenty feet to spare, them nervous ones backed off, pulling on their tethers. But one in particular didn't. She was auburn in color, with splashes of white painted down each leg below each knee like a set of four fancy waders. This one nickered when she saw me. Buffeted her head up and down and whinnied; excited to meet a long, lost friend.

Pa's white-booted sorrel.

Ginny was the pretty mare's name. She looked thin and tired

like the others but came right to me when I kissed twice to draw her near. She nudged and about knocked me over, brushing her lips against me and licking my hands and face. I laughed, wiping the wet away, and hugged her, pattering sweet, soft words into her ears to tell her she was loved and with family once again.

Then Evy shouted a warning.

"Riders!"

I pulled Ginny's picket pin out of the ground and quick led her back to the Chuck Wagon where Luke and Walks-Like-a-Feather were stuffing provisions into our saddle bags.

"I'm getting my horse," Evy called, sounding anxious. She disappeared down the far side of the rise where she'd been watching.

Luke saw me leading the sorrel while he was cinching down a pack and gave me a frown. "You didn't want food, but a horse is fine? I thought you had a problem lifting belongings off these killers and thieves."

"Ain't no problem to it. This is my pa's horse."

My Robert noticed Ginny too. He blossomed with delight, stomping and hawing in a burst of donkey enthusiasm.

"That burro needs to quiet... those riders will hear him," Luke worried.

The sorrel became nervous, sensing fear and excitement, and seeing people she didn't know. But I got her to hurry to Robert, and both settled right off as old companions do. I tied Ginny to string behind him and my borrowed ride, Midas.

There was gunfire in the distance. Walks-Like-a-Feather vaulted onto his gray and motioned for us to do the same. Evy reappeared on the rise to the north.

"You best get your fannies up here!" she hollered. "Something bad going on out there."

CHAPTER 22

WE RODE OUR mounts hard up the slope to meet Evy near the top. Soon as we got there, a mix of rifle and pistol fire popped off again. Two groups of men on horses were a quarter mile out on open ground shooting at one another. The only horse I recognized without a doubt was Marshal Harry Sturges' seventeen-hand dapple.

"I don't understand," said Luke. "I thought any posse coming would be gunning for us."

Walks-Like-a-Feather settled the quandary. "Ten riders on the right, four to the left. One group's the law seeking us, no doubt. But I'd wager the superior force is Little John and his cadre looking to eliminate the law."

"Dapple is on the left," I confirmed, swinging off Midas to pull the spyglass out of Robert's pack.

"That'd be the marshal."

"Indeed, Luke," agreed Walks-Like-a-Feather. "He's here for us."

"Mister Thomas, I think one of the fellas with him is Josiah Thorndike," said Evy. "He owns a draft horse and it's a big-un. Least as big as the dapple you left at the livery, Miss Mae."

I climbed back up in my saddle to get a better view through the telescope. "Drop them formalities. Call me Mae, you hear,

Evy Guntersen? And yeah, it is Mister Thorndike," I said, my eye glued to the lens of the spyglass. "That trail boss Jim Butler is with him. The fourth looks like the Ogallala Sheriff."

As soon as I said it two more shots rang out. Sheriff Deaver dropped off his mount like a length of timber and didn't get up. His horse swung back, confused without its rider. There was another exchange of fire between the two groups. One in the larger bunch went down. Opposite him, Josiah Thorndike doubled over but held to his saddle. I shifted the glass again to see Little John on his quarter horse leading the charge against Marshal Sturges, shouting at his boys to finish what they started. Smoke from black powder hung like a haze over the meadow.

Walks-Like-a-Feather drew his rifle out of its scabbard and loaded a cartridge. "Pick one rustler and bring him down, Mae Kepler. One shot. Then we must flee to find better ground."

"Luke," I said, "take Evy, Robert and Ginny and git!" I shoved the glass against my thigh to collapse it and drew the Winchester we'd gotten from Francis. "Run towards the Platte River quick as you can. You'll hit broken ground soon enough."

I turned to see Walks-Like-a-Feather fire and drop one of Little John's gang. "Find a place we can defend, Luke. That is what we need," the Tonkawa called after the boy, cracking open his Sharps to extract the spent casing.

I took my shot, but Midas twitched causing my bullet to hit the horse of the feller I was aiming at instead. The rider tumbled over the animal when it fell. Both slid across wet sod, the horse dead from the hole I'd plugged in its chest – me feeling the bite of regret for killing an innocent animal in my haste. The rider I'd missed struggled to stand and limped to catch one of the empty horses that lingered amongst the confusion of the engagement.

Little John and the other rustlers broke away when they realized Walks-Like-a-Feather and I had the advantage of height and were shooting on them too. Marshal Sturges used the distraction we created to swing from the ambush, leading Thorndike, and Jim Butler into a stand of sagebrush in the opposite direction. Once there, the three kept on, making it clear they weren't about to let us get away.

Almost at the same instant, bullets from Little John and his rabble whistled through the air with more striking the ridge.

"We are everyone's target now!" Walks-Like-a-Feather growled. "We must move, Mae Kepler." He leaned from his mount to grab my reins, pulling me and Midas off that rise with him. I dropped low in my saddle to not get hit, sheathing the repeater as I did.

Halfway down the slope, Walks-Like-a-Feather let go and kicked his horse into a gallop. I retook my reins and shouted at Midas, "Hup, hup!" Getting him to race after the gray and on south to catch Luke and Evy, who were already a hundred yards gone.

Because Luke was leading Evy and stringing the donkey and Pa's sorrel behind, it didn't take long for us to catch up. It felt good when we reformed a line with them and followed Luke down a narrow gulch that had been cut into the prairie by run-off and rain. The rocks and mud slowed us, but the cut was framed by bare trees and green juniper - cover to obscure us from the *two* bands of determined men now wanting to pursue us. I looked at my companions – Luke and Evy ahead, Walks-Like-a-Feather to our rear, and realized I'd truly gotten them tangled in something worse than what I thought I'd first ridden north for — simple justice.

I no longer knew what that reason had become. Vengeance or some kind of redemption?

As we rode quiet and low together to get away from all them men and guns, I settled on the notion that I'd arrived in Nebraska to receive some portion of each.

"Should we circle back and see about Mister Thorndike?" Evy asked as we threaded between fifteen-foot-high walls of sediment, ice, and rock. Her voice and the troubles within it pried me away from my own vanities. "I... I don't want that poor man dying on account of us," I heard her declare.

Luke's horse slipped and splashed in the icy stream bed as he drove us along the unfamiliar way leading my donkey and Pa's horse. Evy's words made me worry too about the stockman who'd helped us at the grange. We would not have found the outlaw Francis without Josiah Thorndike.

"Maybe young Miss Guntersen *should* return?" Walks-Like-a-

Feather said to me, his horse now very close to mine. The gray stallion made less noise and had an easier time with the rocks and wet terrain. "You can ride your father's sorrel now, Mae. And we have another long gun to use, instead of Evy's Henry rifle."

She and Luke both pivoted in their saddles to see how I might respond to Walks-Like-a-Feather's suggestion, but I offered nothing in return.

The cut we followed took us another hundred and fifty strides to where it entered more open ground. A place where a wash on our right led back to the prairie above. Or where we could stay the course below and ride on through the culvert, remaining hidden from the two groups chasing us.

For me, the choice was a clear one.

"Hell… I'll go," I said, believing I should be the one to return to address the dangers following us and try to convince Josiah Thorndike to return to where a doctor might tend to his wounds. My actions had stirred the hornets' nest we now found ourselves trying to escape. And those same decisions had largely caused the hurt of the men who'd suffered back on the field of battle we'd escaped not moments before.

I tugged at my reins, pulling Midas away from the line, thumping on his flanks with the inside of my boots to goad him out of there and on up the wash.

"Mae?"

Walks-Like-a-Feather knew what I was doing. "Don't be foolhardy!" his voice called after me over the clatter of my mount hoofing up broken stones and soggy soil.

"Mae Kepler!" Luke shouted as well, thinking the same when he saw me pull out of the cut for the prairie above. "Goldarn it."

Walks-Like-A-Feather told Luke and Evy to keep on. "I'll get her," I heard him promise as he rallied after me.

The Tonkawa's gray was strong. That stallion muscled up to flat ground and caught me at the top. Walks-Like-a-Feather snatched my reins, yanking us both to a stiff halt.

"I don't need no chaperone, Thomas." I said, jerking loose, whirling Midas to face him. "Ain't no need for you to face a hangman's noose for something you had nothing to do with."

Walks-Like-A-Feather shifted in his saddle a moment. His

133

expression revealed a rare moment of uncertainty - maybe knowing any words he uttered might somehow be misjudged by me.

With a sigh he spoke his piece. "You and I are in this together, Mae Kepler. Especially now that I've joined your outlaw ways. You might recall me beating on a deputy sheriff and locking him in his own jail cell so early this very morning."

I felt the heat of my anger drop and I ushered Midas closer beside his gray. "Suppose you did, at that."

When I offered the hint of a smile, Walks-Like-A-Feather's face softened but grew serious in his next breath. "Little John is coming, Mae. And we both know two guns are always better than one... whether we're facing murderers and rustlers or a US Marshal. It's your guess who we're about to run into up here first."

The answer appeared not forty feet from us. A big dapple pushed through a stand of young loblolly pines.

"Oh, you'll need more than two guns. No doubt," said the rider on the horse.

US Marshal Harry Sturges.

Seeing him before us made my heart pound with a fear that our run together was about to end there and then. Sturges sat tall in his saddle, despite his left arm still being bound tight to his chest by a white cotton sling. In his right he cradled a 10-gauge shotgun - both barrels pointing at me and Walks-Like-a-Feather.

Mister Thorndike and that Jim Butler edged out between them same saplings, flanking the marshal like twin hounds guarding a rooster.

The three of them rode to close the gap between us. Butler with a Henry rifle, and Josiah Thorndike wearing an old .36 Caliber Colt holstered at his hip. I couldn't tell where he'd been hit, but the stockman didn't look good. Blood soaked down one leg of his trousers and his face was pallid, like his health had all but drained out of him.

I put my hands up where the men could see I held no weapon. Walks-Like-a-Feather did the same. "You here to hang us, or come to help?" I asked.

Harry Sturges touched the brim of his hat, "Ma'am." He

gestured at Walks-Like-a-Feather too, before giving his reply. "What started out as delivering a simple Court Summons, Miss Kepler, ended in a bloody skirmish with those I suspect are the rustlers who killed your Pa."

"Oh, there is no doubt in my mind it's them," I said, my hands balling into fists.

"Little John and at least seven others, last we counted," added Walks-Like-a-Feather.

"Sheriff Deaver alright?" I asked.

The three men looked down, answering my question.

"We were gonna keep going, but Evy Guntersen was worried," I said quick. "Especially about you, Mister Thorndike. Thomas and me come back to convince you to get out of here, sir. I don't want another decent man dying on my account."

The stockman slumped, like he were lost on his mount. Jim Butler sheathed his rifle and reached to prop the man up.

"You're outgunned by hard men who mean to kill," Butler said.

"We'll find cover and finish this," replied Walks-Like-a-Feather. "Please lead Mister Thorndike out of here and get him the help he needs."

When Thorndike heard his name again, he seemed to come out of a haze. The man took off his broad Bollman hat, looking at us. "I plead for you to send the Guntersen girl back too. This is no situation for a child," he said.

"I been thick in it for nearly two weeks, Mister, and I'm but fifteen. Evy is young, but I believe she's a girl who's been through a wagonload more than any of us might care to know. Leaving is a judgement for her alone to make."

We heard Little John and his rabble coming. A half dozen or more men trampling on horseback, probably not far past the trees growing along the culvert we'd followed south.

"Best go now if you're taking this one to a doctor," I told Jim Butler, who quick rooted in his kit then passed me a small sack of ammunition that would fit the caliber of Evy's Henry and the '66 Yellow Boy we'd gotten off Francis.

"Josiah," Butler whispered to the stockman. "Put on your hat and hold tight."

"Stay in the saddle," Walks-Like-a-Feather told them both. "And Jim Butler... please keep safe."

The trail boss removed a glove and Walks-Like-a-Feather did the same. They held each other's gaze a moment while their hands intertwined in a firm clasp. "You as well, Thomas," replied Butler before he led Thorndike out of there at a swift pace west where they could pick up the main trail back to Ogallala. Marshal Sturges watched until they disappeared through the scrub. Walks-Like-a-Feather and I started pivoting our horses to flee back down the cut we'd run up, though Sturges still had us pegged with his 10-gauge.

"You coming, Marshal?" I said. "Be a shame to not put that elephant gun of yours to better use. I am certain we'll need it soon enough."

"Damn right, I'm coming. Still need to serve my Summons."

CHAPTER 23

IN NO TIME, the three of us coaxed our rides down into the cut again. We swung to follow Evy and Luke and found them not far - waiting beside a pool of clear water where the horses and my donkey took a drink.

Luke showed his discomfort when he saw Marshal Sturges with us but was decidedly polite. The two nodded in recognition of one another. I figured that would be it, until Luke shifted his horse and reached to shake the man's hand. Evy followed, leaning off her saddle to give Harry Sturges a hug. "I'm glad you came, sir," she told him.

"You unharmed?" he said.

"Not like I was abducted or nothing. It was my choice to ride out here, sir."

Seeing Evy Guntersen hold her ground against the likes of a US Marshal made me even more grateful she'd asked to ride with us. Made me wish I might always be as brave.

"Well," replied Sturges, him interrupting my spell of admiration. "Your uncle ain't happy."

"I expect not. But these folks here been nothing but kind," said Evy.

The marshal dropped the matter and seemed to drop his concern on it as well. Took in our surroundings, mud walls rising on either side of us. "Got to get out of this trench. If those boys find us, we'll be like fish in a barrel. We need a spot where the ground will let us set our terms. Improve the odds. And that's not down here."

"We're all ears if you have something to suggest, Marshal, sir," said Luke. Of course, the boy glanced at me soon as he spoke. I knew we needed to skedaddle, so my lips stayed buttoned, and I didn't spout-out any more coarse observations about them ears of his.

The marshal spurred his dapple to pass and took the lead, sharing his plan as he did: "A place some folks call the Crown is what I suggest and where I believe we need to be. It juts up a hundred feet or more with exposed boulders for cover. Water will be pooled near the top from all the recent snow and rain."

His big dapple looked jittery, like the animal anticipated what the lawman wanted. "First step is to get out of this ditch, then we'll ride hard for seven, eight miles. Maybe draw these brigands farther from town in the process. You'll know when we're close. The roll of the plain will break and begin to get rougher."

"That's nearly to the Platte," said Walks-Like-a-Feather.

Sturges nodded. "You're familiar with the ground then."

Walks-Like-a-Feather looked back at me and Luke from his saddle. "The place he speaks of is near where we met the Cheyenne."

Sturges started leading deeper into the culvert, speaking over his shoulder at us. "I don't know anything about your Cheyenne friends, but the Crown is the place where we're going to muster control of the field again and put them boys in the ground where they belong."

Walks-Like-a-Feather followed him straight off. Luke untied the lead from his pommel that was stringing Robert and Ginny behind him. "You take these two," he said, passing me the rope. "I've done enough shepherding this day. I'd rather ride drag and watch the pretty scenery from behind for a change."

I took the rope from his hand. "Oh, you would now? What scenery might that be?"

He glanced at Evy and back at me. "Young Miss Guntersen's professed to be but thirteen, Mae. You are the only vista I'm interested in beholding."

The boy made me blush despite the circumstances. He touched his hat, offering a stupid grin this time. "I do like it when you blush."

Before my cheeks turned completely crimson, he waved me on. "After you, Mae. It'll be fine sucking in your dust and sweet perfume for a turn."

I admit, that's when I rolled my eyes. "Hup," I said to Midas, to get him running after Walks-Like-a-Feather and the marshal. Away from foolish charms. Luke, meanwhile, waited for Evy to tuck her horse in line behind me, my donkey and Pa's sorrel. Then he followed in haste on our heels.

Sturges got us up on exposed ground again where we ran hard south with barely a break except to allow our animals a pause to drink. We pushed them mounts to run even swifter when we heard the unmistakable sounds of horses coming on, and the calls of the outlaws who rode them still determined to catch us.

After crossing so much more ground Marshal Sturges pointed to a spot up ahead where a prominent hill did rise before us, a crown of stone at its crest exposed like a jagged ring. A rutted trail broke off and ran through a dormant meadow to snake its way to the top.

"You sure that's a hundred feet high?" I called to Marshal Sturges as we rode. "Looks barely half."

"Been a while, Miss Kepler. Memory does have a way of making things more impressive than the truth. What is important is that the hill is defendable and a decent place to camp. The formations up there will help keep the weather off us too - despite the height."

"We'll let's get on up," hollered Luke from the rear. "I really need…"

There was a thump like someone striking the boy's chest with a clenched fist. Luke gave a gasp, and the crack of a rifle rang out from our rear. Evy screamed a moment later like she'd been bitten by a rattler. Her horse faltered. The sounds of two more shots followed.

"Luke!" I shouted too late.

All hell broke loose. Folks hollered, Robert hawed in fear, nudging close, and our horses started to trampling. Walks-Like-a-Feather gave the call to scatter: "Ride to that hill, or they'll cut us down here and now!"

He spun on his gray and smacked my ride on the bum as he passed, making Midas leap towards the marshal who grabbed the gelding's bridal and had the both of us galloping at that hill whether I wanted it or not. There were more pops and shots and bullets whizzed close. I knew Robert and Ginny were slowing us down, so I cut their string. The donkey and horse peeled off, fleeing together towards the river to get away from the din of the gunfire. Me praying I'd somehow find them again.

If I survived.

Midas ran fast and I dropped low against him, feeling his mane in my face, and calling for Luke. Worried something was dreadfully wrong. When I looked back, it was plain Walks-Like-a-Feather knew what needed to be done despite the shooting. He galloped to Evy, grabbed her about the waist off that dying horse, plopping her in front of him on his. Then he snatched Luke's lead and swung both animals around, his stallion pulling the bay, them galloping after us with the boy flagging behind in his own saddle, barely holding on.

Eight riders broke from the brush and charged like a line of cavalry. They fired as they came, their bullets punching through the grass all about me and the marshal. I can only thank God it's no easy task to draw a bead on a man and ride hard at the same time. Especially through tall grass and uneven ground.

"We got to stop," I cried at Harry Sturges over the thunder of our running horses. "Ain't no way any of them'll survive without us shooting back."

He heard me and released my reins. Pulled sharp on his. I grabbed mine again and did the same. The marshal came to a dead stop - that horse of his was a fine thing. The dapple cut tight, right around to face the men coming, Sturges letting loose with his forty-five revolver. I overshot, on account of me not being as good. But I got Midas swung around and drew the Winchester rifle.

"You got to shoot, Mae!" the marshal shouted. "I'm just making noise with this pistol!"

I levered a round, aimed, and fired, ejecting casings eleven times until my magazine ran dry. Shooting left, then right, then left again past Walks-Like-a-Feather, Evy and Luke. It didn't matter that I only hit but one man and shot another's hat clean off. Me and the marshal, we scared the hell out of them rustlers. They broke, wheeling away, cursing and whining as they did. Little John cussed them all the way back across the meadow to the line of brush where they began.

"Go!" Walks-Like-a-Feather shouted as he and Evy galloped by with Luke trailing. There was blood on Evy's leg, and I knew Luke weren't good at all. His face was ashen, and blood was soaking into the front of his coat, and more dripped from his saddle across the flank of his bay.

Marshal and me followed full on to the base of the hill where Luke teetered out of his saddle and fell into the grass, moaning where he lay.

I shouted, telling Walks-Like-a-Feather to keep on. "Me and the marshal will help Luke!" The Tonkawa glanced back long enough to see I was unharmed and to check if them men were still coming. He rode on, holding Evy against his chest with one arm, pulling Luke's rider-less horse after him up the trail to the top of the Crown and out of sight.

Sturges jumped off his dapple before the horse had stopped and knelt to check the boy.

I followed, squatting beside him. Luke looked at me with a face full of fear, while the marshal used a knife to cut open the boy's Mackinaw coat to see about the wound.

"Load your rifle, Mae Kepler," Sturges told me, but I could not move. There was a gaping hole in Luke's exposed chest, blood and foam oozing out.

Luke tried to catch his breath. Tried to speak. I took his hand and he squeezed. Like he'd done for me inside that jail cage the night before.

"What can I do?" I asked him, leaning close.

"Ride some more... with me... side by side. Us holding hands," Luke whispered softly in return, struggling to draw each

141

breath.

He looked me in the eye. "Mae, don't let... those men... kill another."

I turned back to see about Little John and his rabble across the meadow, worried they'd be coming once more. But as I did, a rifle cracked from above, near the top of the crown. Walks-Like-a-Feather was watching the open ground now too, to keep them outlaws off us while we tended to poor Luke. Only thing I saw was Evy Guntersen's horse Max still dying out there in the middle.

"I promise," I told Luke as I pulled close to him again. "None of them will escape. Not this time."

His gaze held mine for a moment more, then shifted to the marshal. "Sorry about this, sir. I... I wanted to show you... I'm a good lawman... a good deputy."

Sturges drew near now too, speaking in Luke's ear. "Save your breath. I got your badge right here, Deputy Barrientos. Consider yourself Federalized for real. Right now."

Luke's eyes filled wet with tears as the marshal pinned the star back on the lapel of his coat. "You done good. An honest and true detective. Your Sheriff Conley back in Weld told me as such in his affidavit." He patted the side of his long coat. "Got his telegram in my pocket."

Luke smiled. "My sheriff knows... many things... don't he?"

The boy squeezed my fingers ever so slightly again. Closed his eyes.

And left this earth.

There were no sounds in that moment. No horses running, nor shots fired. No shouts to ride this way or that. I felt no fear, and I did not cry.

Not then.

I wish to God it weren't true, but hate suppressed my grief, filling the chambers of my heart, like on that first day after I knew Pa was truly gone. Me setting there beside my murdered dog in the cold damp grass when I swore to find them that done it. I felt the same anger that compelled me to kill the man I believed to be Marshal Harry Sturges and the same potent urge that nearly tempted me to murder the bearded drover back in Ogallala.

My anger made me want to scream. I wanted to run across that meadow to kill Little John and whoever was luckless enough to be with him. Then I looked upon Luke again, my knees pressed against his body. Bloody, silent, and still.

Don't let those men kill another, his voice whispered again, like it was rising off the prairie.

It was time for me to finish this deed. Walks-Like-a-Feather had taught me to cork my temper. I could handle a horse as good as most and knew what it felt like to shoot a man dead. "Load your pistol, Marshal," I said, before standing and slipping the sack of ammunition Jim Butler had given me out of the pocket of my pa's coat.

Sturges took hold of the base of the coat, not wanting me to rise from his side in the tall grass. "This is not the place to make this right," he said.

I pulled free.

"One of us got to put down that horse."

Evy's gelding had begun writhing in the meadow again. Trying to stand, whinnying, and snorting in his struggle. The marshal watched me count the cartridges I snapped into the gate of the rifle I'd emptied. "Twelve," I whispered for Luke once the magazine was packed.

I levered a round, sucked in the crisp winter air and held it in my chest. Aimed at Evy's Max and fired, ending the horse's suffering. I didn't want to lower the weapon, so I held it there a moment, hoping to catch a target I couldn't yet see but knew was there. Little John and his boys now dismounted and cowering in the brush beyond the edge of the meadow.

You are all. Going. To Die.

My vow to cut them down cleared my mind. Allowed me to exhale and breathe.

I squatted again beside the marshal, him saying nothing about the horse I'd shot. He dumped spent casings out of his revolver, reloading fresh ones into five of its six chambers, then holstered the weapon and gazed at me from beneath the brim of his Stetson. "I can't lift this young man without your help. You ready?"

"Might we bury him up there, Marshal?" I asked, with a nod

143

at the Crown.

"If Little John gives us time before he tries something again… I believe that's a fine idea, Miss Kepler."

We drew our two horses close, and I returned the Winchester to its sheath on Midas. I bent low to help move Luke's defiled, rumpled form only to release a dam of sorrow.

It is good to shed tears for the ones we love.

The marshal tried to touch my shoulder, not knowing how else to console my anguish, but I brushed him away. Through sobs I did my best to re-button Lucas Barrientos's bloodied Mackinaw coat, wanting to hide the horrible wound in his chest. I straightened his lapels and swept the dark bangs from his eyes with the tips of my fingers. His sweet face and funny ears made me smile under a wash of memories. And the scent of lye soap and bacon grease lingered when my lips pressed against his one final time.

I tied Luke's hat to my saddle. We draped his body across the dapple, and after, Harry Sturges and I each led our horses in haste up the trail to see about Walks-Like-a-Feather and Evy Guntersen.

CHAPTER 24

NOT LONG AFTER, a bullet struck rock inches above the slouch hat on my head. I ducked, catching the brim, juggling to keep it from tumbling, and from losing my grip on the spyglass I'd been peering through. "Shot came from the scrub oak down across the meadow," I said to the marshal who was crouched near me behind one of the many craggy formations that gave the Crown its name. Some of the stones were waist high. Others twice as tall as a man — all together they formed a ragged ring about us.

"That hat makes a fine target," said Sturges.

"It reminds me of my pa, Marshal. That's why I wear it. Besides, I'd rather get a hole in this old thing, than one in my noggin."

Walks-Like-a-Feather rose from a spot opposite me and the marshal where he'd been re-wrapping Evy's leg with a strip of cloth torn from one of the blankets. "Perhaps present yourself more like a grouse, and less like the mighty eagle," he said. The Tonkawa's words eased a little of the anger I still felt boiling within me. His voice planting my feet more firm on the ground.

Marshal Sturges smiled before skirting across to Walks-Like-a-Feather where he handed him a small flask of liquor. "Bullet go through?" Sturges said to Evy Guntersen.

She nodded; her eyes red from the tears she'd been shedding.

"You pack it tight enough, Thomas?"

"This time," Walks-Like-a-Feather said, with a nod in the marshal's direction. "The wound still wept so I added yarrow and more wad."

"Yarrow's good. That bourbon will sting, but it might help too. Soak that cloth and wrap more after, to keep the outside dry."

While they were fussing over Evy and having a medicinal pissing contest, I set my hat in the dirt and again peered over the stone shielding my form from the outlaws below. "Them boys are coming across," I reported while I gazed down across the fallow field through the spyglass again. "Four, no... five now spreading out. They're making a try."

"We got them right where we want them," said Marshal Sturges.

It was Walks-Like-a-Feather's turn to be amused. He released a chuckle.

"I do not see how either of you find an ounce of humor in our situation," I said, still looking at the rotten drovers now snaking low through the meadow below. "Luke's gone forever, Evy's been shot, and them men out there are coming to finish the rest of us."

I pulled my eye from the glass to look at them. Walks-Like-a-Feather didn't say nothing. The marshal neither. All of us shared a glance at the boy's remains still lying nearby, covered by a saddle blanket on the ground.

It was Sturges who finally spoke.

"I figure it'll be you doing more killing than Little John and his rabble next time we meet. Isn't that what you desired down in that field after they took Luke? Plug a hole in every last one of them."

I swallowed hard, knowing what the marshal said was true. Heard Luke's last words inside my head again too. Making my grief and anger rise once more, like so many dark thoughts muddled about in my mind.

Don't let those men kill another.

"You've learned how it's done, Miss Kepler. This I know,"

Sturges continued as he rose, his eyes upon me. "The killing part is easy. But know there are always consequences to killing a man. Even the ones who require it."

"I... I was angry down there. I'm still trying to contain my anger. But I do see more of the truth of it now." I nodded towards Luke's grave. "This thing with Little John, it's not just between me and him no more. It's not only about the death of my pa and the violation of my ma. It concerns the people and friends I have beside me too. Like in the big war – it's become all of us or all of them."

Marshal Sturges nodded. "Take a look through that fancy glass of yours again, Miss Mae. Watch those fellas come on, for they surely will. But when you see them, remember, who is holding a Winchester."

Walks-Like-a-Feather stood, stepping beside Sturges. "The marshal speaks with honesty, Mae Kepler. We hold the high ground, not them. And if a bullet takes the life of but one, you will provide the rest with something to fear for a time. When you witness them flee, perhaps you'll see the comedy of our situation as well."

I did look, and they were still coming on, much closer than before. I set the telescope against a stone and raised my rifle. Got a bead on the anxious feller in the lead working his way towards us. I hesitated when the scruffy young man in my sight turned to see about the others following him. Held my breath, and when he come full on again, I pulled the trigger. My rifle cracked and the bullet struck square in his chest, knocking him to the ground.

Ending this young man's life felt nothing like what I'd done to the imposter Harry Sturges. I experienced no relief or remorse as the sharp sound of my shot rolled far across the surrounding spaces like distant thunder.

A mere murmur of what I'd done and felt before.

The others coming for us saw him fall dead and froze where they stood. Then ran with a panic – stumbling and zigzagging back across the brown meadow to get away as fast as they could until they disappeared into the tangled scrub oak once more.

"Don't waste another," Marshal Sturges said as he joined me at the natural wall to see what I'd done. "Did that feel right?"

I lowered the Winchester and looked back again at Luke's still form recumbent beneath the saddle blanket.

"Not entirely," I said.

He squeezed my shoulder with his strong hand and then lowered himself down with a groan to sit beside me a moment.

"How'd you and Thomas know them boys would rabbit?" I said.

Sturges looked back across to where Walks-Like-a-Feather sat beside Evy to keep her company while she grieved and ached as well.

"I knew because it's not their fight. It's that fella, Little John's," the marshal said.

"But is it yours either? I mean, after all, me and Luke and Thomas spilled this mess right in your lap."

Harry Sturges smiled.

"I've been in it longer than you and your family, Miss Kepler. I was left for dead out on the same vast prairie where Thomas found you. My horse, my gun and badge… and as fate would have it, even *my name* all stolen. Oh, this is very much my fight too. And, besides, it's my job to be here beside you."

Walks-Like-a-Feather stood again, draping Evy's shoulders with the remains of the blanket he'd used for bandages and moved to a shallow pool of water to clean his hands. "Now that you purchased us a little more time, Mae. Let's use some to set a proper camp." The Tonkawa unfolded the tarp we'd found in Francis' Chuckwagon and glanced at the sky.

I saw it too.

Clouds rolling in to cover the sun as it slipped to the horizon. "Might snow," he said. "If we string it right, maybe this will provide a bit of shelter to keep some of the chill off the horses."

I peered out through the stones again, worried about the meadow and the foul men hidden somewhere beyond it.

"Go help him," the marshal said. "We should take this time to bury Luke too. Those fools won't be back until dark. Not now."

I took him at his word and placed my rifle where I could grab it quick. While Walks-Like-a-Feather and I strung the tarp, Sturges built a simple fire pit with some loose stones for a small fire near Evy's feet. A winter squall *was* coming. The breeze brought frigid air and we could see electricity flashing and dancing, high and wide across a band of black not far off.

When we finished with the tarp and had placed most of our provisions beneath, Walks-Like-a Feather helped me carve a shallow ditch in the earth for Luke. We gently placed him there still wrapped in the blanket and covered the spot with rocks and stones to keep the coyotes and wolves from digging him up.

Evy joined us as we removed our hats and knelt, me leading a short prayer for Lucas Barrientos and his kin while the Marshal watched the meadow below. When it was done, all of us returned to the business at hand. Walks-Like-a-Feather perching himself in a good place amongst the rocks to spell the marshal as our lookout for a time. I checked the horses and their picket lines, thinking of Robert and Ginny again. Knowing there was nothing I could do about them other than believe my donkey and Pa's horse were smart enough to find a place to hunker when the snow arrived.

The Crown was tight like a stiff boot. The circle of large stones shaped a natural defense and provided room enough for us and our animals. "It is a good spot here, Marshal. A little grass and pools of water like you promised," I said, moving to sit beside Evy who still suffered from the wound in her leg. I put my arm around her and she rested against me while the lawman returned to join us with an armload of loose wood to finish building a fire. "Thank you for leading us here," I said to him.

He placed some of the wood in a small pyramid and tucked smaller bits beneath to make it ready for burning. "I am sorry about Deputy Luke. I truly am," Sturges said. "I believe you, he, and I started on the wrong foot."

"Well, I'm not saying it's your fault, Marshal," I said. "But it might've helped if you had given us a chance. Maybe listened a little more before bringing on all your talk of judges, telegrams, and hanging."

Sturges pushed his Stetson back off his brow with a thumb. "Well... I... I was doing what I thought best, and it was late. There were witnesses to be deposed. Didn't intend for anyone to get hurt."

Evy and me watched him finish fussing with the wood for a time until she finally spoke, breaking her stretch of silence. "Marshal… are you planning to arrest Mister Thomas?"

"You mean for beating on Luntz?" Sturges said.

"Well, are you?"

"Sheriff Deaver is dead, Miss Evy. And I got more rank than his deputy Carroll Luntz ever will."

Walks-Like-a-Feather shifted in his spot at the wall. The two men's eyes connected, and Marshal Sturges rose to face him. "That water has flowed under the bridge, Thomas. If Luntz takes up charges, I'll make sure they're dropped."

I felt a small relief, but the Tonkawa revealed nothing, still not releasing his tight gaze on the lawman. "Did you really get a telegram from Sheriff Conley?" I said, remembering what the marshal had whispered to Luke as he passed.

"I did. And I sent a rider to speak to the witness you told me about at Jacobs Ferry."

"You did say you were gonna hang them," Evy said, raising her head off my shoulder. "Heard you say it straight - long before any telegrams and messengers."

"I say a lot of things, Evy Guntersen. Mostly for what you might call *theatrics*. Got to keep folks on their tippy toes sometimes to draw out the truth of a matter with a little more speed." The marshal looked back at Walks-Like-a-Feather. "Sometimes folks speak up. Sometimes they run for cover."

Walks-Like-a-Feather stiffened again, as he held his breach-loader taught in his fists, returning a glare.

"Not saying you're a coward, Thomas. Or a man without honor. Not one bit. You proved that in spades out in that meadow down there. Circumstances force a man to make choices sometimes. I also know the federal badge I exhibit represents a government whose word, when it comes to Indian folk, has been about as reliable as a boat with a hole in it. Like I said, you are a reputable man. One I am proud to stand with."

Walks-Like-a-Feather's grip on the Sharps eased, his eyes softened. Although he offered no reply to the marshal's testament.

"Did you know Luke would die?" I asked, taking Evy's hand

in mine. Wanting something to hold again.

"I did, Miss Kepler. His wound was mortal."

"And you made him a Federal Deputy anyway?" I said, looking over towards Walks-Like-a-Feather. For I knew he was also wanting to see what the marshal might say.

Sturges fussed with the wood for the fire again. Moving the pieces around but not really making any improvements. "I had a child of my own once. A girl named Laura," he finally said. "I know about regret and the importance of words being said before it's too late for their saying. I believe the receiving of that badge from me or even from that other fella supposing to be me... Well, it meant a lot to that young man. Figured it might mean even more to the family he left behind."

Walks-Like-a-Feather joined us, giving a canteen of water to Evy to make sure the girl drank. "I'll finish the fire, Marshal," he said. "And boil us a pot of coffee before it gets too dark."

The lawman stood. Walks-Like-a-Feather handed him his breach-loader, which Sturges took, feeling its balance, checking the load. "He make good coffee, Miss Kepler?"

"If you like it strong," I said.

"Strong is good."

151

CHAPTER 25

THE MARSHAL SET himself between two large rocks where he could watch for signs of Little John as dusk arrived. We boiled water in an old, blackened Dutch oven Walks-Like-a-Feather had packed since my kettle was lost when I cut loose Robert and Ginny. I did have the sack of *Arbuckle's* coffee on Midas, and Walks-Like-a-Feather pulled out his Ma's porcelain cups and saucers wrapped in several wads of unspooled cotton.

He seemed amused at the way my face lit up. "A surprise saved for something special," he declared. "Encircled by angry killers and thieves, what could be more fitting than that?"

"They could have been broken," I said.

"Better such a chance be taken than leaving them in my crumbling sod hut for some foul-smelling prospector to discover."

Marshal Sturges' eyebrows rose beneath his hat. "The man shows style."

"The man's Ma possesses the style," I said. "Thomas is a feller who knows the difference."

Walks-Like-a-Feather grinned at that, which made me happy.

Snow began to fall before darkness fell upon our camp. Walks-Like-a-Feather joined the marshal to guard the approaches to the Crown where the outlaws might attack. And all of us spoke of little things and sipped hot coffee while we waited for them scoundrels to make their move.

I brought Evy's rifle to her by the fire and set mine again where I could reach it, then checked with my hand for the 1848

152

Colt Dragoon, reassured that it was still nestled deep in Pa's pocket. Evy patted the spot beside her, and I sat. She put her arm around me while I warmed my boots against the hot coals.

"You got cartridges?"

"Course." Evy said. "Ain't shot nothing yet."

"Are you feeling okay?"

She turned, looking at me with her bright eyes. "My leg hurts and my stomach's empty."

"Well, if we get through this, I'll fry up some fresh dodgers with salt pork. You can thank that fellow Francis for that."

She smiled. Then leaned close to my ear and whispered. "Mae, I got to pee. Been holding it for a while."

I looked around for a good place for her to do the deed and called softly to Walks-Like-a-Feather. I could barely see him and the marshal through the falling snow, only illuminated by the small fire. "Thomas, I'm gonna help Evy answer nature's call. We're going behind the horses, so don't shoot."

"You have a gun?" he asked.

"Got my pistol. We'll take Evy's Henry too."

"Alright," Walks-Like-A-Feather said. He nodded at the marshal, who agreed as well. "Might be movement out there, so make it quick."

I helped her stand, and she cussed, feeling the pull of the hole in her thigh. We moved around the picketed horses. Evy placed her rifle in the snow behind Midas and Luke's bay. She hiked up the tails of her long coat and dropped her dungarees, relieving her bladder while I balanced her with a hand on her collar. It was cold and still, and the snow fell steady now, making the grass and the rocks of the Crown look pretty and clean.

Course hearing Evy letting loose like a running brook, gave me a strong urge to do much the same. So, I did.

I unbuttoned the bottom few loops on Pa's coat and peeled down Ma's riding britches - me leaning on Evy and her pressing back so neither of us would waver. Harry Sturges' tall dapple on the other side of Midas nickered. Stomped a hoof. Then all four of them animals started clamoring. Which seemed strange until I saw a drover pass to my right, coming out of the rocks with a drawn pistol, walking silently towards the center of our camp. I put my hand across Evy's mouth to keep her from speaking as another appeared on our left doing the same. Neither seemed to notice two young women squatting in the dark.

Evy's eyes grew wide and notions inside my head began to tumble and race.

A rifle cracked. From the sound, I knew it came from Walks-Like-a-Feather's breach loader. He must've taken a shot at something he'd seen down in the meadow on the opposite side. Almost immediately, Evy and I heard the hammers of three, maybe four pistols being set.

"Ain't no need to reload, Injun," a voice spoke from the dark. One I'd heard before.

Not Little John's, but the third feller who'd visited our farm ten days prior.

Frank.

"You and the marshal set them pieces on the ground and put your hands where me and the boys can see," he said.

"No cause for concern," I heard Marshal Sturges reply loud and clear.

"Oh, no concern. None at all," said Frank. "Being that there's more of us than all of you right about now."

My teeth clenched and I stood in silence to pull up my trousers. Helped Evy button hers and I gave her that Henry rifle. She hid between Midas and Luke's Bay, while I drew the Dragoon and followed the footprints of the first man I seen. Me creeping around them horses towards the campfire.

Through the dark and in the flickering light, three drovers were pointing their irons at Walks-Like-a-Feather and Marshal Sturges. The lawman had set his 10-gauge in the snow at his feet and was slowly slipping his .45 out of its holster with two fingers to set it down as well. A fourth outlaw, the one I figured must be Frank, took Walks-Like-a-Feather's rifle and struck him in the gut with it, making the Tonkawa double over with a grunt.

Frank dropped the breach-loader and drew his own pistol, pointing it at Walks-Like-a-Feather's head as if to shoot.

By then I'd tamped down my fears and used the soft snow to hide my intentions. I stood behind the nearest drover, cocked the hammer on the 1848 Colt, and pressed it to the back of his head.

"Might want to ease up on that hammer, Frank," I announced. "That man's a friend of mine." Course I only supposed that the feller farthest from me was the one I knew as Frank. Since I'd never actually seen him.

And it was.

Frank eased his pistol from Walks-Like-a-Feather's head, uncocked it, and turned to see who was telling him what to do. None of the other drovers chose to move or make a sound.

Odd thing was, Frank smiled when he saw me.

"You know who I am?" I said, with a rising disquiet that I'd somehow misjudged my advantages.

"Ain't never seen you. But I do know the fella standing behind you pointing a Spencer at your pretty little skull."

A repeater levered and the tip of its barrel shoved into my back.

"That's a hell of a piece for a young lady such as yourself to keep," said Little John from a step behind me. His voice not much more than a whisper in my left ear. "How about you ease up on *your* hammer, missy. 'Fore I split you in two with a ball from my rifle?"

I released the catch and relaxed the hammer.

Soon as I did, the first drover I'd been pointing it at spun and shoved his pistol in my face while Little John shouldered his Spencer and took my Dragoon. John forced me down on my knees, walking around to look me in the eye.

"Thought you were a man in them clothes, but you got such a pretty voice. Course your face ain't much better than last time we spoke."

He took his finger off the trigger of the 1848 Colt and struck me on the cheek. The pistol's long barrel knocked me sideways, tearing open the skin there. I felt no fear in that moment, only stiff pain from the side of my face. And the recollection of deep loss once more as I witnessed Pa's hat tumble off my head into the snow beside me upside down.

"Wonder if you're as good a whore as your mama was?" Little John said before he pulled me by my hair to raise me on my knees again. "I don't know how you did it, but I do believe you killed young Bobcat." He looked at his men all about him. "Bitch killed

Francis too."

"She did no such thing," said Walks-Like-a-Feather from the opposite side of the Crown, still bent before Frank.

"Don't say nothing," I sputtered.

But the scoundrel Frank was quick and jabbed his empty fist into Walks-Like-a-Feather's gut, making him fold over a second time.

"Oh, you're next, Injun," said Little John. He put his left hand under my chin squeezing, planting his face close to mine to where I could smell the Rye on his breath. Then dug his fingers into the torn part of my cheek. I saw the fire flickering in his eyes before he shoved me backward into the snow again, pointed the Army Dragoon at my chest, cocked its hammer and pulled the trigger.

"No!" I heard Walks-Like-a-Feather shout.

There was a loud bang and flash and a lot of smoke. I felt a .44 caliber ball bump against my chest. But it made no wound and I weren't dead. The expression on Little John's face reminded me of the feelings I'd had the first time I tried to kill the bogus Harry Sturges with that same shabby pistol.

From that moment on, all sorts of misery came to call.

Evy Guntersen's Henry rifle cracked from inside the picketed horses. The gunman standing beside Little John had his face shot open in a spray of skin, blood, and bone.

Little John swung his hand out wide to set the heavy hammer on my Dragoon a second time. But the marshal dove for his 10-gauge, lifted it, and fired, blowing off Little John's hand. Taking the 1848 Colt with it.

Frank struck Walks-Like-a-Feather in the forehead with the butt of his pistol knocking him cold. He spun, remembering to cock the weapon before shooting Marshal Sturges, who cut him down in return with a blast from his second barrel. I watched Frank fall lifeless into the snow as I heard Evy begin to lever and fire that Henry of hers some more. She dropped at least one more of them drovers before I could get on my feet again.

Snow swirled and there was smoke hanging everywhere from the black powder being discharged, making it even harder to see. Little John screamed, him staring at the shreds that remained of his missing hand, while the last gunman yet unscathed took him by his good arm to flee. The Spencer rifle John had shouldered clattered to the snow because he didn't have no fingers to hold it by.

I got mine around it as them two leaped away through one of the natural gaps between the stones. Shot off one round but wasn't sure how to rearm the tricky repeater because its action don't work the same as a Henry or a Winchester.

Dismayed, I cast the thing aside and scrambled to see about Marshal Sturges and Walks-Like-a-Feather, while Evy Guntersen hobbled to the wall, taking more shots in the dark at the two men running.

CHAPTER 26

BY THE TIME I got to Marshal Sturges, he was sitting upright and had already begun to cuss. "Damnation, that Frank. The bastard put another bullet in my lame shoulder."

"Well, he's nothing to nobody no more," I said. "You seen to that."

The outlaw had taken a full load of 10-gauge buckshot in the gut. Ripped through his long coat, shirt, stomach, and intestines so you could see clear to his spine at the back.

Frank was dead when he hit the ground. Both he and Francis were now gone. I felt no pity for them two who'd chosen to violate my ma as I laid hog-tied in the bed of our buckboard wagon - no way to help her or stop them.

The snow deepened, and Walks-Like-a-Feather's face was planted in it. He weren't moving, so I shifted my attention, rolling him on his side, making sure he was still breathing, which he was. I heard Evy sliding cartridges down the magazine tube of her Henry somewhere in the dark at the far edge of the Crown.

"Get over here when you're done reloading, girl," I shouted. "There's no need to shoot no more. The last of them rogues have run off!"

Evy limped to where we could see her again. There was snow sprinkled in her hair and more on her shoulders. She was holding that rifle tight and had half her riding coat stuffed into the back of her dungarees. When she realized dead drovers were on the ground around us, Evy started to cry. "I killed them, didn't I?"

"Most of them," said Marshal Sturges, looking at the three men bleeding in the fresh snow. "I got to say it, Miss Guntersen, you are one hell of a shot."

The compliment didn't help. Evy stuck the butt of her rifle in the snow, used it to lower herself down, and sat with her bad leg stretched stiff to sob even worse than before.

"Come on Evy," I said. "You're gonna get all wet and cold. Can't have you crying no more about this. I need your help getting Thomas under that tarp. The marshal too."

She took off her gloves and used her fingers to rub her eyes, then slung the Henry across her shoulder to help me drag Walks-Like-a-Feather out of the weather. We propped him up with one of the saddles and covered him with wool blankets. Marshal Sturges got there on his own accord, keeping that shotgun with him. I found his .45 in the snow and gave that to him as well. He sat close against Walks-Like-a-Feather under them blankets so the two would warm each other while I looked at the bullet wound in his shoulder. Sturges told me what to do. How to clean and pack the hole, then dress it and put it back in his sling while Evy got a new fire going closer to the tarp.

"I'm going after Little John," I declared after suitably wrapping the angry gash on Walks-Like-a-Feather's forehead. The words Luke said before he died were repeating behind my own. And the promise I told him I would keep. *Don't let those men kill another.*

Evy looked at me.

"But it's night. And you're leaving me here with all these dead men?"

"I'm not dead yet, little Miss," the marshal said. He used his good arm to touch Walks-Like-a-Feather's cheek with the back of his hand. "And this decent fella isn't either."

"I know. I didn't mean it in that regard. It's just, what if some of them rustlers come back?"

"There's barely two or three left," I said. "You helped make certain of that, Evy. Them boys will not return before I discover them first. Besides, you got the Henry, and, like the marshal says, you're not one to miss."

Sturges lifted his 10-gauge to remind Evy it was resting right there in his lap. "Oh, we'll be fine," he assured me. "Can't say I'm certain it's the best strategy for you to keep after those fugitives without help. That Little John is like a hurt bear now. And he's got at least one other able drover out there with him. If it don't feel right, you leave them be, and we'll figure another way to get this done."

I didn't want to think about the dangerous part right then. Only the vows I'd made to Luke, and Pa, my ma, and to Mister Coates. So, I pulled the skillet, some salt pork, cornmeal, and lard out of our chuck sack.

"You know what to do with this, right?" I asked Evy.

"Course I do. I know about more than just shoeing horses and shooting guns. Besides, you think my uncle really had anything to do with cookery?"

"Then I'll leave you to it."

The marshal called to me as I stood. "Before you go, I need three things of you, Miss Kepler." He winced as he spoke, pressing his hand against the wound at his shoulder.

"I wish I had something for that. Thomas used the last of your whiskey on Evy's wound."

He gave me a stiff smile and looked at Walks-Like-a-Feather lying next to him, who still showed no sign of rousing. Sturges used his one good arm to tug on the edges of the blankets covering him, tucking them tighter to keep out more of the cold.

"What about them three things, Marshal?" I said with a little too much impatience.

He adjusted himself to sit straighter, "Coax the horses in here - all of them except my dapple. The cover will help keep them out of the snow and they'll keep Evy, Thomas, and me a little warmer."

"Not the dapple? You saying you want me to mount on him again?"

He nodded. "If you're going out there alone, you need a bigger, faster, stronger horse. And mine cuts better than any I ever seen."

I didn't know what to say until I remembered he mentioned

he'd wanted something more.

"Yes, my ledger. That's the last. Bring it here if you would. It's in my bag over yonder."

I tucked him better, like he'd done for Walks-Like-a-Feather. Found a picket spike in the gear and drove it in the ground near the back of the tarp. Then I got him the ledger, and brought Luke's bay, Midas, and Walks-Like-a-Feather's gray stallion under the edge of the tarp and tied them all to the picket. I quickly saddled the dapple and secured my Winchester in its scabbard.

Before I got in the saddle, I remembered Pa's hat and retrieved the Slouch from where it lay beside a dead drover on the ground. The snow had filled it like flour in a bowl, which I dumped before placing the hat on my head.

"Mae!" the marshal called as I put one foot in a stirrup. "I got something else to give you." I suppose I sighed before returning under the tarp to kneel beside him. "Evy," he said while she was fussing with the fire again. "I can use only the one hand, so need you to do this for me."

He passed her an object I couldn't yet see. Evy's face bloomed. She turned, took hold of the left lapel of my pa's coat, and pinned a silver circle and star to it. Words stamped into the badge with no uncertain terms: *United States Deputy Marshal.*

"I... I don't understand."

"I need to deputize you. Make it legal. Since I can't be there when you take that man down."

I looked at Walks-Like-a-Feather, lying there in a deep slumber. "Maybe I *should* wait. Thomas would be a better lawman than me, surely."

"By the time he wakes, them men will be gone. And I don't believe I am allowed deputize him."

"Not allowed? Thomas is a man, which I ain't. And he's more level-headed, and a far better shot than I'll ever be."

"It is troublesome, I do not disagree. But Thomas is Tonkawa. So, if you're going, I need to deputize *you,* Mae Kepler. Right now."

"Mae, you can do this," said Evy. "I know you can." She placed her hand over her mouth, staring at me like I were suddenly someone grand.

"But I'm only fifteen."

"Stop digging ditches," said Sturges. "You already decided you're going after them. And you can ride and shoot and exhibit no fear when the chips fall. I need a temporary deputy, and you are it. There must be an officer of the peace present to make an arrest or a killing proper in the eyes of federal law."

I swallowed hard, my fingers touching the badge Evy had pinned upon my person as the marshal scribbled in his ledger. He made me swear an oath, making sure I repeated after him careful, and word for word.

"You're telling me I'm actually a U.S. Deputy Marshal. Right now. In this moment?"

"Just like I done for young Luke, but more proper. You are official for thirty days. That's how long I sanctioned the appointment for." He handed me the leather-bound log to read and told me to make my mark beside his brief notations. An entry for Lucas Barrientos was the last before mine:

12 Nov, '73. M. Kepler, Weld County, Colorado Territory. +30.

"Thirty days, Miss Mae Kepler. Or least until a district judge learns you are underage and truly not a man."

CHAPTER 27

MARSHAL STURGES' TALL dapple carried me down the rutted trail to the meadow and the scrub beyond. The snow had stopped falling, but clouds remained above for the moment. Once the horse took me beyond the last dim shadows cast by the campfire, we were plunged into an icy darkness. There was no moon and no stars to light our way. Even the distant flashes of lightning we seen near dusk were long gone.

I urged the dapple across the landscape as best I could. He sniffed the snow and walked and sniffed again, moving forward for a time with a certain caution until I no longer knew where I was. The open space, endless beneath a blanket of white and all that black above, became bewildering. I couldn't tell north from south, east from west until there came a ragged scream. Someone in desperate pain hollering in the night, followed by a long string of curses and a single flash and sharp pop.

The light and report of what sounded like a pistol shot ignited the prairie. For a brief second, I saw the indentations of horses' hooves, covered and faded, but still marked in the snow. The flash gave me and the dapple a point to reckon and the chance to pursue the men we sought farther into the gloom.

We stumbled on at a slow walk, the brave horse growing more and more unsure. I became afraid of injuring him somehow, like I'd done to poor Janey. Not wanting to make the same fool mistake twice, I finally dismounted to lead him, instead of the other way 'round. Taking hold of his bridal, moving forward again one step at a time, praying we'd not stumble into some unseen culvert or frozen wash.

A break appeared above. A gap in the clouds where the faint shine from stars seeped through to reflect off the snow. I could sense the faded tracks again, and beyond, not sixty yards on, I perceived someone standing out there on a bleak patch of ground.

A tall, stout man, dark and wearing a hat and a broad riding coat.

I stopped, afraid to continue. Retreated along the flank of Marshal Sturges' horse and slid the Winchester out of its scabbard. I levered a round, holding the butt of the rifle against my hip with one hand, the stock wedged against the inside of my forearm and elbow. Then took the dapple's bridal again to cover the rest of the distance between us and the tall man who still hadn't moved.

The clouds opened more, and I began to realize the man was not alone. There was someone fallen in the snow beside him. And that's about the time it occurred to me the tall man wasn't a man at all, but a horse facing directly towards me as it stood silently in the snow.

I walked faster, covering the rest of the distance still leading on foot. The lone horse nickered, and it became apparent that what I thought had been a riding coat was only a wool blanket draped across its back to keep the weather off and the animal warm. That hat I'd imagined was merely the animal's ears poking wide and listening for danger in the dark.

Them clouds kept moving and separating, allowing more stars to light upon the landscape. I pulled my scarf tight about my ears and neck. Pulled the Slouch hat down low and felt my toes inside my boots grow cold as the temperature dropped.

There was a man lying face down in the snow beside the

horse. An empty pistol rig had been cast there with him. Along with what looked like a length of twirled and blood-stained cloth that had been left as well. The man's body had been stripped of most everything. His hat, overcoat, gloves, and boots were all gone.

Wanting to discover what might have happened, I re-secured the Winchester in its scabbard, removed one of my own gloves and knelt to make sure the drover was truly dead. He weren't breathing, but his body wasn't cold. When I rolled him, there was a single hole in the center of his chest. And when I stood again, I spied multiple sets of tracks coming and going from that spot. All were fresh and left by more than a half dozen horses who'd gathered and moved on. I knew this because none were tempered by the fresh snow that had stopped falling not thirty minutes prior.

The abandoned horse didn't fuss when I took him and tied him to the pommel of my saddle. I stepped to remount the dapple and realized another figure had emerged out of the dark from the direction I'd just walked. A man wearing a curious sombrero and riding a familiar, sturdy stallion. Moving silent and steady towards me across the prairie's dim coat of white.

Walks-Like-a-Feather weren't especially happy with me.

"What are you doing?" I asked before he had the occasion to raise the same question.

"Making certain the woman doesn't get herself killed."

"I ain't gonna let that man get the best of me," I declared. "He'll be in irons before he gets a chance."

Walks-Like-a-Feather rode close to where I could get a decent view of him and the bandage I'd wrapped about his noggin from side to side. A dark stain seeped through the place where he'd tamped the cloth beneath the band of his dreadful hat. "You shouldn't be out here," I said. "That Frank about cracked your skull in two."

"I am ashamed to think I let him defeat me," the Tonkawa replied. He looked down at his gloved hands clutching the gray's reins. When he raised his chin again, I saw his frustrations. "I am angry, Mae Kepler... Dismayed Harry Sturges sent you alone on such a dangerous, fool's errand."

"The marshal did no such thing. I chose the deed myself and it ain't no fool's errand. Like I said, I plan to catch Little John and finish this thing between he and I." I nodded at the frozen prairie and some of the tracks leading away. "He is there. *And I will catch him.*"

Nothing happened for a moment until I placed my boot in the stirrup and swung my leg over the dapple to ride in the saddle again. I cut the horse in a tight circle to face Walks-Like-a-Feather and his gray, thinking it was funny how the two proud ponies got along so well – sniffing and kissing each other the way horses do when they greet – despite me and him being somewhat agitated with each other. "Is the marshal okay?" I said, after a pause.

"Sturges was sleeping when I left. Evy is doing the guarding. That young lady is wide awake and ramped mighty high on coffee."

"Lord. And me worried all this while about abandoning them."

Walks-Like-a-Feather reached out to stroke the face of the lawman's horse from his own saddle. "That choice has passed, Mae. You and I are here now. So, tell me what you've found."

I showed him the dead man in the snow, and the tracks coming and going every which way from the spot. He dismounted to examine the prints. "I see many riders and several empties. Mules maybe... pack animals for sure. I believe two groups crossed this place."

"Them tracks looked clean to me. Laid down since the snow stopped."

"They tell a simple story, and you've learned to read it," he said.

"So, why didn't they take *him*?" I asked, motioning at the abandoned horse, still draped in his blanket, and tied to mine. Any horse had value and weren't a thing to be discarded or left behind without reason.

Walks-Like-a-Feather circled round. Checked under the horse's blanket then ran his hands up and down the animal's legs to feel for injuries. He only spoke after he'd lifted each of its hooves, one by one. "He's thrown a shoe. Foot might be injured, or he might have run in fear to hide in the dark and returned to

166

this spot after the others had moved on. No matter the truth, it makes no sense to leave him here for wolves to find. We'll bring him if he can walk, and I'll replace that shoe when daylight returns. I keep spares and nails for such a purpose."

We identified the groups coming and going. Three with two pack animals rallied before they rode west in a single line. Four more horses fled south towards the Platte.

"Our choice is obvious," said Walks-Like-a-Feather. "Cheyenne riders took to the west, each following the other with resolve.

"So Little John and what's left of his rabble rode for the river," I said.

Walks-Like-a-Feather nodded. "Their only choice was to get away."

We pursued the outlaws south under the light of the stars, riding side by side for a time. The horse I'd found strung along behind and seemed content enough despite the loss of a shoe. We moved at a deliberate pace, not wanting to come upon the rustlers without intention. The landscape sloped and we dropped into a broad floodplain - the last stretch before the Platte.

The sounds we heard were few. The crunching of fresh snow beneath our horse's hooves, the creak of taught saddle leather stiffened from the cold, and, not long after, a pack of coyote howling and yipping somewhere from the direction we come.

Them coyotes were distant. Probably closer to the marshal and Evy Guntersen at the Crown than nearer to us. I knew their guns would ward off any pack that might appear in the glow of their campfire.

An icy breeze picked up. We began to hear the flow of water. And when gunfire erupted without warning, Walks-Like-a-Feather and I jumped from our saddles to squat in the snow to wait and watch. Silhouettes of mounts and riders were lit from the flashes of their shots. Men called to one another, and vague shapes of horses broke to the right and to the left in the flat space between us and the river.

Walks-Like-a-Feather urged silence and caution with his hands. He led me and the dapple and that lost horse on foot until we discovered another corpse in the snow. This one propped

167

against the carcass of his mount.

I assumed it was another of Little John's rabble, but Walks-Like-a-Feather knew the difference. "Cheyenne," he whispered.

The dead man seemed fancy, like a feller who might have come from one of the gambling halls in town until we got close. He wore a tailored wool coat and scarf, that covered homespun woolens beneath. His hair was long and dark. Two thin braids framed his face, each adorned with a feather. An oversized, flat-brimmed hat was plunked on his head like it didn't quite fit. Both he and the horse, a lanky, painted mustang, had been shot multiple times. The blood spilled wasn't yet frozen.

"Rifle's in the snow, here," I said.

"Five are running right," Walks-Like-a-Feather showed me, pointing to hoof prints headed for a distant row of trees stretching to the river.

I pulled myself up into the saddle again and rode the dapple farther along the tracks we'd been following while he took a closer look at the dead mustang and man. "Thomas," I called, after covering only a short distance more. "There's another here and more tracks."

"Coming," he answered, and we examined a third body in the snow.

This was a drover who'd taken a ball to the face. The marks left around him told us part of his story. The feller's mount seemed to have survived but had been nabbed along with the pack animal tied to it. These were led in a direction same as the first five we seen.

"The Cheyenne are claiming the horses," said Walks-Like-a-Feather. "They may be watching us still. Waiting inside those trees."

"You think it might be some of the same we met coming north?"

"I do not know, Mae. Desperation and the cold of winter, hungry families to feed... all these things will push anyone to do more than they might otherwise."

We mounted to move with greater speed on to the river as a half-moon broke through a last line of clouds scattered at the horizon. The Platte came into view much closer than I'd imagined. Ripples in its rush of water sparkled. Details that couldn't be seen before were illuminated, giving the night a sudden crispness and austere glow.

"Our shadows," Walks-Like-a-Feather whispered with an edge in his voice that hadn't been there before. Too late I realized we'd come to be in plain view of anyone wishing to see.

My skull snapped and I felt a jarring pain. Like someone had struck the side of my head with the handle of a shovel. The force cast me out of my saddle, and I heard the crack of the shooter's rifle before my form crashed against frozen ground.

Walks-Like-a-Feather tugged his reins, rolling his gray stallion sharp to the right to get clear. He swung from his saddle, switching to hideaway style as the rifleman levered and fired three more times. I saw his muzzle flashes through the dark behind the silhouettes of a big old stump and fallen tree. Walks-Like-a-Feather grunted, and he and the gray went down, sliding ten or more feet across the snow. The dapple I'd been riding whirled left to escape in the opposite direction, tugging the horse we'd found along with him.

Leaving me alone where I lie.

My shoulder stung from hitting the ground, and my left ear felt like it was on fire. I slipped my glove off and covered the ear with the palm of my hand, pressing hard to ease the pain. My scarf became saturated with blood, and I could tell my ear was in bad shape. The shooter's bullet had raked the side of my face and gone on, taking a good hunk of my ear with it. I felt overcome by an odd sense of shame and all I could think of was Luke. Me harping on and on, relentless about them big ears of his.

I saw Walks-Like-a-Feather struggling to get out from under his horse. I tried to rise on all fours to help but felt woozy and slumped to vomit in the snow. Ma's voice jabbered in my brain as I heaved. A recollection of her preaching at me over supper about Galatians 6:7.

All the deeds you ever done, Mae. The good and the bad. They'll return to you one day...

For a man shall reap what he sows.

I'm not sure how much time passed when I realized that the ice clumped against my torn ear took away some of the sting. I couldn't hear Walks-Like-a-Feather moving no more.

"You still with me?" I sputtered, closing my eyes, saying a prayer to Jesus. Desiring with all my heart Walks-Like-a-Feather had been spared.

He turned his head to the side to gaze at me and spoke in a calm voice. "The gray is gone, Mae. My legs are pinned beneath."

"You been shot?"

"I don't think. How about you?"

I told him about my face and ear and wanted to cry. I thought of Ma, me aching suddenly to see her again. Missed my daddy and remembered Mister Coates doing all he could to help them and help me on the day this began. I took in a long, deep breath and released it, pushing the air out between my pursed lips. When it was done instead of wallowing in pain and shame, I began to think about the shooter.

Little John would not have missed. Not like that.

That bearded murderer had skill with a rifle at distance and had killed my pa from at least two hundred yards. I remembered him swinging his gun hand out to re-set the hammer on my Dragoon. And the marshal taking that same hand off with a burst from his 10-gauge.

Someone different was doing the shooting this time. One of them other drovers who might not be as comfortable with a long gun.

As that news struck me, the world went dark. A puff cloud drifted to obscure the light of the moon and gifted me a few more moments.

"I'm coming, Thomas," I said. "But something needs doing first."

"Mae Kepler... don't."

I buried my hands in the snow to wipe some of the blood clean and stood, wobbling, still dizzy. Pa's hat was gone, so I pulled my hair off the torn ear and tied it in a quick knot to hang across my opposite shoulder. The dapple came back bringing the stray. I stumbled to them, pattering whispers to keep both calm. Slid the Winchester from its sheath and started at a flat run toward that old stump and fallen tree where I knew them men were hiding.

My feet had covered half the distance by the time the moon broke clear and chose to shine on me and everything else out on the prairie again.

CHAPTER 28

MY RIDING BOOTS were cold, and I slipped and stumbled, dashing across the snow. Blood leaked into my eye from the gash at my temple and my head throbbed something fierce. I figured them men behind that stump were gonna pop their heads up and shoot if I didn't. So, I squeezed the trigger on the Winchester and kept at it - levering, firing, and counting brass casings that ejected and tumbled into the snow as I advanced.

I hammered that stump until the rifle ran dry. When the last shell flipped out of the receiver, I kissed the ground and dug in Pa's coat pocket, spilling a fistful of cartridges on top of the fresh snow beside me.

Someone shot back. Three rounds from a .44 pistol. The bullets whistled and hummed as they ranged over my head. "Missy Mae!" shouted a voice I'd never forget from behind the stump. "Figured you'd come knocking."

"Didn't think you knew my name," I hollered back, firing to let Little John know I hadn't run out of justifications to cut him down and that I had plenty of bullets to do it with.

"Your mama spoke of it."

My anger flared when he mentioned Ma, and I shot twice more in his direction. "United States Deputy Marshal to you, John!"

He grunted a laugh from the other side of the stump. "Yeah, you and Joe Hill."

"Who in heaven's name is Joe Hill?" I said.

"Joe weren't a man planning no rise to heaven. But he was the finest trickster I ever met. A man of many names, Joe kept the ladies wetting their pantaloons and swooning for more."

I reloaded the Winchester and recognized the man Little John described, even though the name was unfamiliar.

Harry Sturges.

Not the genuine article. The young pretender whose true identity I'd never known. I recalled the handsome scoundrel again with tussled hair, half asleep, yet randy enough at the break of day to appreciate the curve of my backside.

I lowered my head to think and catch my breath.

"You are my only interest now," I finally said.

He replied with another laugh. "Well, I like the sound of that, sweet Missy Mae. Got something special waiting."

"Something small to be sure," I said.

No laughter came from his side again. The sky brightened as it does in the last stretch of night before dawn, so I drew nearer. Crawling this time. Using my knees and elbows, keeping the muzzle of my rifle clear of dirt and snow as I did. "Sweet now, am I?" I said, wanting him to say something more – anything for me to know right where he was hiding.

"I never spoke a word of ugly."

I took another deep breath, John's voice feet away, the stump all that remained to separate me from him. I clenched the Winchester: "*Not very pretty* is the phrase I most recall."

"Slip of the tongue, Missy Mae. Your mama gave you plenty for a fella to covet."

He made his move, stood before I could swing my rifle up to drop him. Little John cocked his pistol, pointed it at my face, but lingered when he realized a little too late that he and I weren't the only souls left alive out on the prairie near that old rotten stump.

I fired first, my shot lifting Little John off his feet. At such a range the .44 caliber bullet passed clean through his chest. Two more long guns ignited from yards behind me, one round striking his leg, and the second whistling on by to disappear into the darkness beyond. John's pistol discharged against the ground, and he crumpled backward into the snow.

Walks-Like-a-Feather appeared at my side, hand on my shoulder. Two of them Cheyenne we'd met coming north were with him. They stopped to see if I was alright, then circled about the stump to make sure no one was left behind it to oppose us. The warriors exchanged gestures with Walks-Like-a-Feather, then sprinted to the river where they recovered two more horses that must have been Little John's and the last of his gang now slumped dead beside him.

John was yet alive, breathing ragged and looking up at the sky with dismay in his eyes. His dead companion still held a shiny, new Winchester repeater in the grip of his hands — the outlaw who'd clipped off a sizeable portion of my left ear. I figured I returned the favor when I shot him through his face and neck as some of the bullets I'd used to pepper that stump passed through its rotten remains to finish him.

Little John tried to catch some air as he bled from his wounds. "I... I never laid a hand on your mama," he said. "Frank and Francis done that."

I gave my rifle to Walks-Like-a-Feather as I knelt beside the injured outlaw. "But you didn't stop them. They did what they would and left my ma to die exposed and bloody under our supper table."

John squeezed his eyes shut like he were trying to close off the truth of what I said.

Make sure they ain't breathing when you're spent.

"You told that boy to do the same to me. But he's dead and gone. Like Joe Hill, them two Franks, and all the other luckless drovers too."

I rose, gazing down at Little John and his broken form — feeling no pride nor sorrow.

"You are the only one that remains," I said. "And you, sir, are now in Federal custody for the murder of my father, the murder of Deputy Lucas Barrientos of Weld County, and the violation and attempted murder of my mother."

"Ain't no authority here," he sputtered.

I leaned close to show him the lapel of my coat.

"Well now, Missy Mae... sporting a silver star."

With no more words to speak, I turned my back on him, containing my tears and balling my fists. Walks-Like-a-Feather tried to return my rifle, but I held up my hands. "Don't give me that or I'll shoot that man dead like we done all the others."

"What are we to do with him then, Mae Kepler?"

The sun crested at the horizon to light the snow as if making a million diamonds shine. "Bind his wounds and keep him alive if the Lord will allow it. Shoot the man if he moves," I said, no longer wanting to view his bearded face.

As I spoke, I noticed a Cheyenne woman walking towards us, like she'd come from nowhere, appearing out of the middle of all that bright white light.

Leading a burro and a white booted sorrel.

The donkey threw his head up when he caught wind of me, and the mare tugged her lead and stomped. The woman smiled, understanding the nature of their emotions.

"Robert! Ginny!" I yelled, forgetting a moment about Little John and the troubles he'd brought into my life. All the folks who had died on account of him and me.

Tears of joy flowed instead, and I ran to the woman who gave me their leads and stepped aside, watching me wrap my arms around that donkey and mare, them kissing and nudging me right back. I expect we were the happiest critters there ever could be at that single moment near the boundary between the State of Nebraska and the wilds of the Colorado Territory.

CHAPTER 29

WE HEFTED Little John to ride on Robert E. Lee. Tied his ankles together beneath the donkey's belly and set him on a Cheyenne blanket given to us after we traded all them saddles stolen by his rabble. He was hunched and wrapped in bandages for his wounds, wearing one of the dead drovers' shabby long coats. Walks-Like-a-Feather gave Little John his crumpled sombrero to wear. Our prisoner now had more in common with a sack of turnips than a dangerous fugitive.

He cussed about the burro until I told him if he dared say another word, I'd shoot him where the sun don't shine and drag him back to Ogallala across the snow instead. Maybe save the good people of Nebraska the price of a judge and timber for gallows.

After Walks-Like-a-Feather patched my face and ear, he and I took turns speaking words of remembrance and honor over the gray stallion who'd been such a noble companion. He saddled on Marshal Sturges' dapple for the time being and looked quite handsome in Little John's fancy, wide-brimmed hat. I passed the Sharps rifle he'd carried for so long to one of the Cheyenne without Walks-Like-a-Feather knowing. Then slipped the new Winchester '73 I'd pulled from the grip of the last dead rustler into his rifle scabbard as a surprise replacement.

The Cheyenne gathered the other stolen horses for themselves and butchered the remains of the two dead ones as food for their hungry families. We parted ways much the same as before. Weren't no words exchanged. Only the understanding of unspoken reverence as the Cheyenne rode off to wherever their travels took them after another day was done.

By the time we loped back to the base of the Crown, a wagon had arrived teamed by local men sent with regards from Josiah Thorndike. They brought with them a telegram which presented the brief, but joyful words that Ma was yet alive. Recovering in our home back in Weld County with a certain Mister Lawrence Coates by her side.

My heart leaped and I released an ocean full of tears after so many weeks of not knowing. Walks-Like-a-Feather took me in his arms. Holding me for a time. Finally wiping the wet from my cheeks.

"Daylight's burning," he said with a nod towards the rise above us. "Don't you want to share some of this good word with our two friends who still wait and worry *for us* atop that Crown?"

I didn't want to let go but knew what he said was true. We had a camp yet to break and a long ride ahead of us still. And of course, the news I was now busting to tell everyone. We wasted no time charging the horses up the rutted trail to see about Evy Guntersen and the marshal while the teamsters guarded our prisoner. Up top, we found Evy folding the tarp and Harry Sturges resting against his saddle by the fire. The big 10-gauge still cradled in his lap.

"You able to ride?" I asked him, not wanting to sound too excited, as I swung my legs off Ginny.

"Either of you ever going to give me back my steed?" he grumbled, watching Walks-Like-a-Feather dismount from the big dapple. "Seems to me everyone's getting their fair chance to ride him except his owner." The marshal slumped a little, looking weary and pale. Older in the light of day than I'd remembered.

Then I about burst.

Unspooling the news about Ma and our dearest family friend. And the facts about how we'd caught Little John, who now waited in shackles and under guard in the meadow below.

Sturges' sat up straight again, his mood distinctly brighter. Evy ran from her work to embrace me, gently touching the bloodied patch on what remained of my ear, pressing me tight to her like she figured I weren't never coming back.

"I... I'm so happy your ma is on the mend," she said.

Evy looked at Walks-Like-a-Feather, who'd come up beside me, then brought her bright eyes back to mine. "Happier still that you both returned yet breathing and in one piece as well."

"Mostly," I said, dropping my gaze from hers, thinking again on all the killing we'd done to get to this place. She touched the bandage on my ear once more as if wanting to draw out any last bits of pain that remained. Evy turned to Walks-Like-a-Feather, hugging him almost as long. When she pulled away, Evy looked like she'd just remembered some fact long forgotten.

"I... I found something of yours in the snow, Mae. Something you might still desire."

It was my turn to smile again when she showed me the 1848 Army Dragoon - the piece that had been so untrue, but that had saved my hide more than once. Evy had cleaned the pistol and passed it to me, holstered in a worn rig she must have taken from one of the drovers she'd shot.

"Never thought this old dud was worth keeping until now," I said, belting the piece about my hips for the first time, embracing her once more.

"All this loving and affection," the marshal called with a wave of his hand, getting our attention to return to him. "Seems to me, Miss Mae, it might be time for you to splurge. Buy yourself some fresh cap and ball for that old thing." Everyone laughed at this, feeling a sort of salvation that each of us had survived to live another day and share a little more fellowship together.

I set Luke's lovely brown hat on my head to replace the Slouch I'd lost, and Evy and me finished folding the tarp. Walks-Like-a-Feather switched saddles — placing his on the bay and getting the marshal properly kitted on his own horse once more.

"You're not riding with me to file them papers, are you?" Harry Sturges asked once we helped him back in the saddle.

"The prisoner is yours now, Marshal," I said. "But I do expect you at my supper table with a sizable part of any reward come

Spring."

He tipped his hat. "Be honored, ma'am. Rest-assured, I will arrive with my holes mended and my appetite intact."

I turned to Evy. "You'll be coming too, soon as you settle things with that uncle of yours? There is no doubt I need your skills to get the farm moving in the right direction again."

"You truly mean it?"

"You're a part of my family now, Evy. I hope you feel the same. There is space if you'll have it. Plenty of work and good company." She flashed those eyes and that smile of hers and held me and Walks-Like-a-Feather once more.

I knelt at Luke's grave a final time. Reflected upon the soft moments he and I had shared together. Then whispered a prayer for him and his kin before all of us remaining alive rode down the rutted trail to where the teamsters and prisoner waited in the wagon.

Marshal Sturges and Evy Guntersen led the wagon and prisoner north, back to Ogallala. Walks-Like-a-Feather and me veered southwest across the Platte River. Finally headed somewhere we'd already been for the first time in many days.

CHAPTER 30

WE TRAVELED and camped across two nights. Riding constant from dawn until dusk, mostly deep in our own thoughts, following the main cattle trail through the snow-covered ground. The passage was cut so deep by so many steers it was a hard thing to lose.

Eventually everything about the land, even its smell, grew familiar. Ginny and my Robert seemed happy we were together, trotting along through a mixture of light snow, a stark winter sky, and the constant chill of the prairie breeze. For my part, I was glad to be riding Pa's sorrel, knowing how happy Ma and Mister Coates would be to see me push through our gate leading Robert. Releasing him and Ginny to graze on the slope of the upper pasture once again.

"Did you like that handsome trail boss, name a Jim Butler?" I asked Walks-Like-a-Feather on what I knew would be the last morning of the last day, breaching a silence that had endured for the better part of our long ride from the Crown.

He didn't say nothing back. Didn't smile or frown. Kept minding his horse, pretending like he was busy doing other things like watching the clouds or following a hawk as it flit and circled above us. Our time together was almost at an end, and I wanted to know more about him. Who he was and why I liked him so very much. But I let the question simmer a little longer before I spoke on it again about a mile farther on.

"He was a rugged and striking man. Saw him eyeing you at the Ogallala Grange."

The corners of Walks-Like-a-Feather's mouth curled up at their edges to form a thin smile beneath the shadow of his new hat's broad brim.

"You're nudging about Jim Butler again."

"I am."

"Seemed to be one of the good ones. A handsome man," Walks-Like-a-Feather finally conceded.

"The marshal mentioned Jim Butler's got kin near Fort Davis," I told him as we rode side by side. "Plans to use his stake from this year's drive to start himself a small spread out there."

He said nothing more, so we loped along in the same manner and in silence a few more miles. Traveling across the prairie, observing its snow-covered roll shift and flow like a vast inland sea. Me beside him, knowing that without the fellowship Walks-Like-a-Feather shared with me, and the depth of his wisdom, I would've never survived.

Robert's ears perked like he knew we was getting close. The donkey began to tug on his lead, more frequent than not, wanting to sniff at things he found interesting along the way. Prairie dogs played and darted across frozen ground. The critters would watch as we passed, and then go on back to getting in general trouble with one another by the time we'd gone. Hardy little yellow flowers poked through in spots here and there where the pale sun warmed the earth and exposed some of the rich sod beneath its winter cover.

At last, we came upon a big, rutted trail running crossways towards the State of Kansas, and then opposite, west to where the Colorado front range rose to touch the sky.

"Well, Miss U.S. Marshal," said Walks-Like-a-Feather.

"Oh, shush."

He pulled on his reins, pausing Luke's bay. Took the dark, wide-brimmed hat from his head so he could take all of me in with his eyes for a long moment. He rotated that brim nervously

181

in his hands until he nodded toward the mountains.

"This is where I must turn away, Mae Kepler."

My donkey ambled up his trailing lead to join us, standing between, sniffing and reminding the both of us he was still there. Walks-Like-a-Feather placed the hat back on his head, touched the burro behind the ears to give him a scratch. "I'll not entirely miss you, Mister Robert E. Lee, but you've always remained loyal."

"He is fine, ain't he?" I said with a tight smile, really not thinking about the donkey. Only seeing Walks-Like-a-Feather mounted there before me. Recalling all we'd been through together.

"I *will* miss *you,* Mae."

My eyes burned. Began to tear.

"My ma's house... our home... the door is open to share... ever you need something, Thomas-Walks-Like-a-Feather," I whispered and started to cry. Feeling again like the girl who'd been riding with her Pa and Mister Coates in the back of a wagon on the way to town.

"You are a loyal friend," I said, wiping my eyes on the leather of the gloves he'd given me. "The man who saved me from myself on more than one occasion."

Walks-Like-a-Feather touched the tip of his brim. "You have journeyed far, Mae Kepler, in the time we've shared. Do what you do best. Keep following your heart, for it will always be an honest teacher."

He nudged Luke's horse to turn away. I watched as the bay carried him west at a walk.

"Thomas," I called before he'd gotten too far. "Where are you going anyway?"

He turned to look back at me, two streams of tears rolling down his own sun-weathered face. "Going to see the mountains. Look in on my mother and sisters."

"They'll have you?"

"Can't know," he said a little louder so I could still hear as the distance between us grew. "But I would like to visit with them. Know how they're getting along."

"And after?" I shouted. Not wanting our union to end.

"Never been to Fort Davis. Think I might like to know what that's all about."

CHAPTER 31

THE SUN DISAPPEARED far to the west when the last miles brought me to the edge of Weld. The trail became a street, and Ginny and Robert began to prance as the world no longer seemed wild and strange.

We trotted into town, past Mrs. Johnson's Boarding House, Sheriff Conley's office and jail, the livery, and Hancock's Saloon, which was boisterous of course. Illuminated from within.

Main Street was nearly vacant as we continued through our little town. The Mercantile and Land Office had closed for the evening. Doc Lowry's barber shop too – although I had a strong urge to race up the man's steps to give him a hug and share with him the many tales I had to tell.

But I kept on.

The sky darkened as the road drew past our unpainted church and out onto the prairie once more. It became clear, with stars above lighting our way along the six miles to home. No clouds on the horizon to bring us warnings of snow or foul weather.

Ginny carried me to the crick, leading Robert all the while. Taking us down and up its muddy shores. My heart beat faster as we loped through our family's grove of cottonwoods.

Course I had to stop when I saw daddy's grave — the one Mister Coates had lovingly fashioned for him.

"We got them men, Pa," I whispered. "Every last one."

I said a prayer, and a stillness fell upon me from the night air all around. The crick gurgled soft and sweet a short distance away. I felt grateful knowing all who passed this place might for a moment well remember my daddy.

Ginny shifted, reminding me we weren't yet home. So, I nudged her on for a dozen or more strides, Robert loosening his lead to follow us as close as he could. Until, at last, we came to a place where we could gaze beyond the lower pasture that united the best parts of our farm.

The place where I saw Ma as I remembered her. Busy within the warmly lit window of our small house across the way.

Me breaking into the broadest smile I'd made in far too many days.

ACKNOWLEDGMENTS

Special thanks to my wife who was always supportive of me throughout the four-year process of writing, re-writing, and editing *The Ones We Love*. To my many beta readers including the first brave ones who slogged through a rather rough manuscript – Brian King, Larry McMahan, and John Pierson. And to so many more who shared such wonderful, honest feedback: Lesa, Ken, Dan, Paloma, Sadie, Andy, Ginny, Susan, Bob, Jacques, Carol, Jose, Cynthia, Denny, Barry, Shari, Greg, and Rich.

For my two wonderful editors – PJ (Tricia) Hoover, and Samantha M. Clark – both accomplished, Austin-based authors who spent hours helping me craft a far better novel.

And finally, to Owen Timberlake Kinney and Dr. William R. Kinney, members of the Chickasaw Nation. (Bill is also in the Chickasaw Hall of Fame!) As Native American sensibility readers, each took a leap of faith in me by agreeing to vet my story and its characters for cultural accuracy.

ABOUT THE AUTHOR

Jonathan's background includes a BA in Literature from West Virginia Wesleyan, and an MA from Temple University in Speech Language Pathology. He and his wife have lived, worked, and raised two children in the offbeat, sometimes weird, western culture of Austin, Texas for twenty-five years. *The Ones We Love* is his first novel.

If you've enjoyed reading this journey with Mae Kepler, help spread the word and take a moment to post a book review on Amazon and/or Goodreads. Thanks!